The Peacemaker:

THE YASHAR PURSUIT

#2 THE
PEACEMAKER
The Yashar Pursuit
Adam Hamilton

A BERKLEY MEDALLION BOOK
published by
BERKLEY PUBLISHING CORPORATION

SBN 425-02636-1

*BERKLEY MEDALLION BOOKS are published by
Berkley Publishing Corporation
200 Madison Avenue
New York, N.Y. 10016*

BERKLEY MEDALLION BOOKS ® TM 757, 375

Printed in the United States of America

Berkley Medallion Edition, August, 1974

Chapter One

The single spotlight swept the flat prairie in a wide arc as the battered gray van turned off the dirt road. The driver stretched his neck, gripping the wheel tightly as the truck bounced and rattled over the rutted ground. He growled. "Damn prairie looks flatter'n it is."

He swore under his breath at the small circle of light allowed him. The searchlight on top of the cab was manned by Bill Scoey. It made less light than headlights would.

Jake Stacton threaded the van through patches of bunch grass and greasewood. The truck wheels spun occasionally in loose sand. Beside him the stocky Red bounced on the seat. The young kid, Willy, was silent, holding on as the van lurched heavily. Willy was sitting in the narrow space next to the specially built rig of steel with its heavy canvas straps. The rig was deeply padded to form a kind of nest. Willy kept his foot braced against the locked wheels of a large dolly lashed to the side of the truck. Each of the men cradled a rifle in his arms. Behind, on the floor, were submachine guns. All four men had gas masks dangling from their necks.

Jake slowed the van as the searchlight cut out. That meant they'd be at the wire fence in less than a half mile. They were close enough now to be sighted by the patrol if it came early.

Dropping to a lower gear, Jake swore again. The moon had already crossed the ridge of buttes in the

5

west, but there was enough light to make out the slight rise of the land. He turned his head. "There it is."

Red and Willy shifted, muttering. The truck stopped and Red grunted and swung the metal door outward and jumped to the ground. Willy was behind him, gazing in all directions, extracting wire cutters from the lineman's belt he wore. They laid the rifles at the base of the fence and began cutting the wire along one of the supporting poles. The barbed wire fence was seven feet high, angled at the top and ridged with loops of barbed wire. Jake sat hunched over the wheel watching them. The snapping of the taut wires was loud in the quiet night. But Pringle had said it would be a cinch.

Scoey climbed down from the top of the cab. He crawled inside the truck, swearing in the dark, and came out slinging the strap of one of the submachine guns over his shoulder.

It took ten minutes to cut through the fence and tie back the sections of wire, making a gap large enough to drive the van through. Red signaled Jake who moved the truck forward slowly. Red walked ahead, guiding the driver by moving his arms and Jake found himself clenching his jaws because of the noise of the engine.

Then he saw the rows of waiting cylinders. Red made a circling motion and Jake swung the wheel. He backed the van around and up to the first of the cylinders with Red guiding him. It was damned hard to do at night.

When he halted the truck he set the brakes and jumped down. The three others already had the gas masks over their faces; Jake pulled his into place. Red manipulated the hydraulic hoist, bringing it down almost level with the ground. Red motioned and three of them got behind the first cylinder, prying with long steel bars.

Jake could hear Red muttering in the mask. The cylinder moved—it was heavy as hell. More than half a

6

ton, someone had said. But it was round. They got it moving, rolling—kept it rolling. It grated on the hoist and clanked. Scoey had the curved blocks ready, shoving each under the canister. Red waved them back and the hoist moved upward. Jake sighed with relief. Pringle had said it'd be no trouble. It was going like clockwork.

He followed Scoey and Willy inside the truck to the hoist. Red was prying the inner block loose. They rolled the canister to the rig and levered it into place. Willy and Red began fastening the straps. Scoey went to the hoist and got the back doors of the van closed.

Red stripped off his mask. "All right, let's get the hell outa here."

"Get the rifles," Scoey said.

Jake found them on the ground near the front tire and passed them up to Scoey as he climbed back to the cab. Jake swung behind the wheel and shoved the truck into gear. His heart was hammering, not only with the exertion. The clock on the dash said they'd done it in twenty-five minutes. The guard patrol was due in another five.

The patrol car always came around from the right; it made a run past this stretch of fence every half hour, give or take five or ten minutes. In the three days they'd checked intervals, the car had been on time only once. Usually it was a couple of minutes late.

Jake followed the tracks back to the gap in the fence. The truck lurched and bumped heavily. The goddamn canister weighed like hell. It made a difference.

They almost made it.

Jake had slowed to a crawl, in lowest gear, to ease the van through the hole in the fence when a light flashed behind them. Jake saw it in the rear view. A guard had spotted the truck. Red and Willy yelled together.

Jake gave her the gas. Cursing, Red scuttled to the

7

door on the right, opened it, and leaned out with one of the rifles. Holding it awkwardly in his left hand, he fired a shot.

The wheels spun in the sand and the truck jerked to a halt. Jake gunned the engine and nothing happened. He saw Red staring at him as if it was his fault. "Goddammit, we're stuck!"

Red swore. He pointed at Willy, "C'mon, gimme a hand." He jumped to the ground. Willy followed, growling under his breath.

Jake kept gunning it. He could hear a horn blaring far behind them. Jesus, what a crock if they were caught because they got stuck in the sand! He was sweating inside the mask, and ripped it off. Red and Willy were doing something out there, yelling at each other. Red stopped once to fire a clip at the distant patrol car.

Jake stared out the window, seeing lights. The first bullet came whining over the cab and he ducked involuntarily. He heard Scoey scrambling down. It would only be moments before the guard came rushing them. The damn horn would alert everyone within a mile. A siren began wailing. More bullets came, searching for them.

Scoey stood on the fender of the truck and his submachine gun stuttered. Red yelled at him. "Knock off the goddamn shooting!"

"I'm tryin' to hit the light!"

"You're doing a lousy job!"

Jake gunned the engine again and this time the wheels took hold. They rolled out of the sand.

"Ever'body in," Red yelled. "Let's go—"

Jake held the wheels straight, heading directly away from the fence. Red clambered onto the step, one arm locked around the door frame as he tried to pull it shut. His face was flushed, full in the glare of the Army searchlight. He leveled the rifle and another shot roared

8

out. The truck lurched, bouncing and rolling.

Jake barely had time to glance around as Willy and Scoey came tumbling in. Willy had a submachine gun; he looked pale as a ghost, teeth fixed in a grimace. He was the youngest of them all and was probably scared to death. A hail of bullets whined past, several rattled on the side of the van.

Gradually Jake turned the wheel; the road was off to the right he guessed; he could no longer see the tracks they'd made coming in. It couldn't be far, maybe three quarters of a mile—how long would it take the Army to organize a pursuit? The bullets still came at them and Red fired back, emptying the rifle.

"Can't hit the goddamn light," he growled.

Willy stood in the doorway, bracing himself. He leveled the chopper and got off a long burst. The light went out and plunged them in sudden darkness. Willy laughed, a harsh cackle, as Scoey pulled him inside. Bullets spanged the side and rear of the van but didn't penetrate the reinforced steel panels.

Jake turned farther to the right. A new hail of bullets rapped into the metal. The outside rear view mirror shattered suddenly as armor-piercing slugs shattered the doorframe and went on through the windshield leaving starred holes.

Willy yelped, doubling up and dropping the gun. He clawed at the door and slid to the floorboards with Socey grabbing at him. "They get you, Willy—?"

Jake shot a glance at the other. Scoey had a flashlight out and bright red blood was everywhere. Willy seemed covered with it. The light winked out as Red growled. "Move it!"

The truck jerked forward in a burst of speed, jolting over the hummocked ground, then Jake let up. The canister in the back was full of deadly poison gas. He dared not rupture it.

9

Willy was groaning, slobbering words. Red and Scoey lifted him into the back end where they could lay him down.

Jake got the best speed he could out of the hulking van. Bullets still sought them out, but fewer now; they were a much poorer target, only a hazy blob in the darkness. The spot had been carefully picked. It was three miles to the nearest gate where most of the Army vehicles were kept. By the time the Army got a pursuing force after them they *should* be long gone. Pringle had thought so—but then, Pringle wasn't here.

It had taken hard study, but Jake had memorized an elaborate, twisting route, over prairie and back roads, that would take them clear of the Point Archer Chemical Warfare Depot in the shortest possible time. The military had no helicopter closer than Grafton and they wouldn't use it at night anyway.

He looked over his shoulder at Red. "He gonna be all right?"

The stocky man only grunted. He came up into the cab and stared out, unzipping his jacket.

Jake said, "C'mon, how is he?"

Red's hand came out with a snub-nosed revolver. "No, he ain't gonna make it. How far's the road?"

"Pretty close."

Red grunted again and went into the back once more. Behind them the gunfire had died out but the keening sound of the siren still reached their ears. Who the hell was there to warn except the depot? There wasn't anyone in fifty miles. Why the hell didn't they shut the damned thing off now?

There was the road. Jake slowed and turned into it, bumping over the shoulder. It was hardly more than a twin track in the hardpacked earth but it was level. The van rode smooth all of a sudden and Jake let out his breath. They were home free. Sure as hell. Jake pressed down the gas pedal. For several miles the van sped in an almost straight line before it turned again and headed cross country. But even in the sand the going was easier here. They would reach another road in two miles.

Red spoke in his ear, "Pull up, Jake."

"What?"

"You heard me, for crissakes, don't argue!"

Jake sighed and let up on the gas, applying the brake. The wheels of the heavy van bit into the dirt. They ground to a halt, engine running. Scoey got out and opened the rear doors, shoving and pounding them because of the bullet-torn uprights. Red was grunting, heaving Willy. Scoey took the man's head and between them they muscled Willy to the ground.

Jake asked, "What the hell're you doing?" He turned and stared. Red shone the flashlight on Willy, whose eyelids fluttered.

"Christ—it—hurts—"

"Yeah, kid," Red growled. "I know."

"Help m-me—" Willy's breath was rasping harshly as he struggled to breathe.

"Sure, kid," Red said almost gently. He raised the snub-nose and fired into Willy's temple just below the blonde hairline. The sound of the shot was a sharp crack. Willy's body jerked and slumped. Red got up, sliding the pistol into his belt.

"Jesus!" Jake gasped, eyes staring. "You killed 'im!"

"Let's go," Red growled.

Scoey scrambled into the van, lips pressed tight.

"Move it!" Red yelled, jumping into the cab.

Jake got the van into gear and the truck lurched. "What'd you kill 'im for?"

"He was as good as dead. Th'way he was spurting blood he wouldn't last another hour. He'd'ave slowed us down." Red settled back against the cushion. "C'mon, push this thing."

The first shot startled Corporal Eddie Conners from the half doze he'd fallen into. He jerked forward in the swivel chair, glancing around the small office in the quonset as if expecting to see the cause of the disturbance close at hand.

Another shot cracked, unmistakable this time. Eddie's hand slapped at the buzzer on the desk. The soft beginning growl of the alarm bell filtered from the barracks. Eddie thrust both hands into the desk drawer. Where the hell was his pistol? He found the pistol and belt and ran from the office.

A half dozen partly dressed men were pouring from the barracks. The horn was blaring and the siren was beginning to wail. What the hell was going on? He ran across the compound toward the edge of the stockpiled tanks that marched in precise rows, stretching into the black night toward the distant perimeter of the fence. A bright searchlight threw a beam over the humped shadows, giving enough light to see along the corridors between the rows. Eddie ran with the naked pistol in his hand, the breath tightening in his throat.

He'd been on duty in this Godforsaken outpost for three months. This was the first time anything louder than a cricket's chirp had disturbed his watch. Shots! They meant trouble, no way around it. But who the hell would be fooling around the depot? Sergeant Crawford had reported everything quiet as a forgotten cemetery only an hour ago.

The shots continued, coming from the north fence. Another burst of automatic fire shredded the night. Eddie glanced behind him. The men were coming, cussing and yelling. He motioned to them to spread out.

He came to the end of the row of canisters. Pressing against the tanks, he peered into the darkness. In front of him a lighted flashlight lay in the weeds, the beam showing a thin path in the dust. Several yards beyond, a man lay motionless. Eddie crouched and moved toward the figure, making sure he stayed out of the light. The figure was in uniform. Eddie switched off the flash and put his back to the fence. With fingers squeezed over the glass, he switched on the light and stared.

It was Greg Crawford!

Eddie rolled the Sergeant over and felt for a pulse. The man was alive but unconscious. There was blood on his chest.

From the compound a searchlight scanned the fence. The bright beam stopped abruptly when it snagged on the opening that had been cut. Eddie glimpsed a large van lurching away over the desert. He raised his pistol and fired five times at the van.

A burst of machine gun fire answered and Eddie dived to the ground. Swearing, he crawled away toward the canisters, dragging the wounded man with him.

A half dozen soldiers were running toward him. Eddie shouted an order, telling them to spread out, pointing at the last man, "You—c'mere."

"Hey, who'zat?" the man asked.

"Sergeant Crawford. You go get a medic out here, quick."

"Anyone else hurt?"

"I dunno—get moving!"

The man sprinted off into the night. Eddie felt again for Crawford's pulse. Still good.

He crouched by the supine figure, listening to the battle. He could no longer see the mysterious van. A dozen soldiers were wasting ammo, firing into the night. Then someone stopped them and yelled at them to assemble.

Lights went on along the fence and Eddie stood up, putting the pistol on safety, thrusting it into the holster. He wondered if he'd hit the truck. What the hell was it doing here anyway? He bent and tore Crawford's shirt away so he could look at the wound. It was bleeding hardly at all, an ugly puffy hole in the chest.

13

Behind him, someone yelled. Eddie turned, frowning. Had they missed some of the raiders? He reached for the pistol.

Then he saw the guy stumble. There were five or six guys maybe a hundred feet away along the row of canisters. The man fell, kicking and jerking. Eddie started forward, then stopped short. Another of the men staggered, then three more were down. Another raced from the tanks, hands over nose and mouth, his rifle tossed away in panic.

Eddie backed, his face suddenly pale. He knew instantly what had happened. A bullet had ruptured one of the canisters! Deadly nerve gas was escaping.

Then he ran back to the fallen Sergeant, scooped him up, and began running heavily toward the compound.

Colonel Henry Billingsley strode into the small conference room at the end of the Administration Building.

The three men grouped about a table glanced up. All of them rose quickly. Billingsley said, "Ease, gentlemen—"

Captain Judd Rockland pulled out a chair for the older man and resumed his own.

"What the hell's happened?" Billingsley demanded. He sat, watching Rockland motion to the two enlisted men; they moved outside to the corridor, closing the door.

As the lock clicked, Rockland said, "There was a break-in tonight at the Point Archer Depot, Colonel. Damned well organized. We're not sure how many men were involved, but they got away with a cylinder of M-34 GB."

Billingsley looked shocked. Then he scowled. "Got away! Lord, man, didn't you track them down?"

Feet shuffled. Rockland shook his head. "We deployed every available man, sir. By the time we got on their trail they were too far ahead for us to catch up.

We're not sure yet where they went. The entire thing was planned down to the most minute detail."

The colonel snorted. "You can't go across that desert without leaving tracks!"

"No, sir," Rockland said evenly. "They left tracks. They cut across to Olley Road, then went across the open desert to Highway Five. From there on it's anyone's guess."

Billingsley pounded the table. "We've got security there!" He got up and paced to the door and back; face red, scowling. "A canister of gas?! What the hell!"

Rockland said, "I've called for help. The air force will start searching at daybreak, sir. They've got one chopper and some light planes . . ."

"How the hell did they get in?"

"Cut the fence, sir. They must have had a special rig to get the canister out—a hydraulic lift, I suspect. That'd be the easiest way."

"Jesus, there's going to be hell to pay," Billingsley growled. He stared at them. "Any casualties?"

Lieutenant Ingelow said, "A number, sir. Five dead that we know of—"

Billingsley whirled. "Five?!"

"A canister got ruptured, sir," Rockland put in quickly. "They fired off a lot of stuff. The wind was blowing away from the compound otherwise—" He shrugged. "There're a half dozen men in the infirmary, a few with bullet wounds."

"We'll have 'em in the hospital here by morning," Ingelow said.

Colonel Billingsley paced to the door and back. He was a tall, rangy man with a fringe of graying hair around a tanned bald head. For three years he'd been the Commandant of the Grafton Military Reservation, an Infantry training post sixty-eight miles from Point Archer. Rockland had gotten him out of bed with the news. Point Archer had notified Washington and an immediate call had been relayed to Grafton. A team of investigators was on the way.

"One canister of gas?" Billingsley asked. "Just one?"

"Enough to cause a hell of a lot of trouble, sir."

Billingsley shook his head. "I don't like that damned stuff. What about Point Archer?"

Rockland said, "Emergency crews neutralized the whole area. There's no danger there now, sir. But too late to help the poor bastards who were on the scene."

"Any of it blow into town?"

"No, sir. It couldn't come this far. Besides, the wind was blowing the other way." Rockland noted the Colonel's obvious relief.

"All right. Clamp a 'top secret' on it. No one's to know." He looked round at them. "No one. The information is not to go outside this room. Is that clear? When the gas cases come in from Point Archer, quarantine them . . . with MPs."

"Yes, sir."

"And get that search moving in the morning." Billingsley scowled again. "Why the hell would anyone steal a canister of gas?" None of them answered him. He grunted and went out.

Rockland received another call from Point Archer in a half hour. Captain Haynes was on the line.

"Rockland? Can you send me some troops? We've had two more deaths . . ."

"From the gas?"

"Yes. They had too much of it to hang on. The orderly thinks their nervous systems were badly damaged. Couldn't get the heartbeats back to normal. Your doctor hasn't arrived, by the way."

"He ought to be there any time now." Rockland looked at his watch. He'd sent off the doc and his aides almost an hour ago.

"I think they were scared to death, too," Haynes

16

said. "Not that I blame them. Usually if we can keep them breathing for twenty minutes we have it licked."

"What about the gunshots?"

"Not bad, except for Sergeant Crawford. He took one in the upper chest. We think he'll put through."

"I'll send you thirty men, okay?"

"All right."

"The Colonel has put a top security rating on the whole affair—"

"Yes, we got the same instructions from Washington. No press, nothing. Thanks, Rocky."

"You bet. Any little thing." Rockland hung up and sighed. Jesus, a canister of nerve gas! Now what?

Chapter Two

Franklin Trask, short, chunky, and balding, looked up as Vera Crawford entered the office. He saw at once that she was pale—there was something wrong. He indicated a chair, "What is it?"

"Something's happened to Greg." Vera dropped into the chair and took a deep breath, trying to compose herself. "I just got a call from him."

"Then he's all right—he can talk anyway."

She nodded. "He's in an Army hospital in Utah. God, Frank, it gave me a turn, hearing his voice. I mean he sounded weak as a kitten."

"What happened to him?" Frank Trask was in his shirt sleeves, half-glasses perched on the end of his nose. He reached for a smouldering pipe and stared at her. Vera was Barry's private secretary, a gal who worked best under fire. Nothing ever ruffled her. He was surprised to see her shaken up . . . she and Greg had been divorced four or five years.

"He wouldn't tell me. Some kind of accident, I guess. But Greg is one of those indestructible types. You don't expect to hear . . ." She sighed and shook her head. "Vicky has been looking forward to seeing him."

"Hmmm." Frank blew smoke. He remembered Greg Crawford as a husky man, a big tanned specimen, a career soldier. Long separations had played havoc with the marriage and it had finally gone on the rocks. But he and Vera were still on good terms and their daughter, Vicky, spent several weeks every year with her father. He said, "Well, can't you just postpone Vicky's visit?"

"She's terribly upset, Frank."

Frank looked at the end of the cigar. Vera hadn't come in here to tell him that. Kids got upset but they got over it. Maybe it was Vera who was mostly upset. He cocked his head at her. "So what can I do for you?"

She smiled very slightly. "Get me some time off."

"You mean you want to go out to Utah?"

"Yes."

He grunted. Vera was a fine looking woman, as level headed as they came, but she must still have a thing for this man. Vera hadn't remarried and he knew for a fact that a dozen very good proposals had come her way. She was blonde and tailored, enormously efficient, but the office would survive if she was away for a few days. He nodded.

"All right, a couple of days." He ground out the cigar.

"I can't understand why he'd postpone Vicky's visit, unless he was really bad. That's what worries me."

"I suppose he told you he was all right, not to worry?"

"Of course he did."

Frank Trask sighed. He was married himself. Naturally she wanted to take the kid and chase out there to sit at his bed and boss the nurses. Women are like that. Even Vera. Even ice-in-the-veins Vera Crawford.

"All right," he said. "Take off. I'll square it with Barry."

Frank Trask got up and put his jacket on. He patted his pockets to see that he had his pipe and glasses and went out and along the hall to Barry's hexagonal office.

Rapping lightly on the side door, he opened it and

19

went in, bypassing the secretaries' offices. Barry was standing at the window looking out over the rolling Pennsylvania hills. He was wearing a light blue open-neck shirt over gray slacks and looked as tanned and fit as always. Barrington Hewes-Bradford at thirty-two was one of the youngest and shrewdest financiers in the world—and one of the richest. HB enterprises girdled the globe. Franklin Trask was his chief of staff.

"Afternoon, Frank," Barry said, turning. "I hear Vera is off to someplace in Utah."

It was a statement and a question at the same time. Frank nodded. "Her ex-husband is in the hospital there. Some kind of accident. Vera feels that if she's there she can hustle up the white corpuscles or something. You know how she is."

"Greg hurt? What happened?" Barry thrust hands in pockets and cocked his head. He had a hawk nose and black hair. There was always an air of restlessness about him, as if he might take off at top speed, in some direction, any second.

Frank sat down and fiddled with the pipe. "Vera doesn't know. They wouldn't tell her, and Greg tried to discourage her going there. But Vicky wants to see her father—" Frank shrugged and lit the pipe.

Barry nodded. "Well, if we can help, do what you can."

"Right." Barry meant with money or hired help, maybe even with a little clout if necessary. Vera was one of the family, almost. She had been with Barry seven years and was one of the few "irreplaceables." She was super efficient; she ran her office with its half dozen secretaries and typists like a drill sergeant and she had a fantastic memory.

Barry said, "Now, about the Ludgate thing . . . fill me in on our progress." He went behind the big teak desk and sat down, putting his feet up on a rolling file.

"It's halted dead center," Frank said. "The senatorial

committee is holding secret meetings on it and a couple of other contracts. I'm told we'll have some kind of answer in maybe a week." He looked at the bowl of the pipe and fished for matches. "Unless you can speed that up a little."

Barry smiled. "You mean Senator Troyer?"

"Affirmative. His committee has been sitting on it." The Ludgate contract was a routine matter. An HB company in the west was manufacturing certain machine components and had been for several years. Suddenly Senator Troyer, a notorious fussbudget, was peering into the fine print with his bifocals, in search of newspaper headlines. Troyer loved to make investigations pay off in headlines slightly in advance of his coming up for re-election. The Ludgate contract was probably one of the most honest on the books. Barry was interested because they had stockpiled materials for the continuing program and HB would suffer a loss if they were not used as planned.

Barry made a note. "I'll see what leverage I can use on the committee." He found a cigarette and tapped it idly on a thumbnail. "I'm invited to sit in on Joe Westerbeck's conference on reforestation in a couple of days. I might go down to Washington; take care of both at the same time."

Joe Westerbeck was Secretary of the Interior. Frank nodded. Barry's contacts were amazing; he was even on a first-name basis with the President who had been here to the mansion in Pennsylvania a number of times.

Frank got up. "There's nothing else pressing. In fact it's almost too quiet. Maybe I'll take a few days myself."

Barry smiled again. "I wish you would, Frank. Let Bert worry with the office for a week. Take Sara up to Maine."

Frank puffed the pipe, gazing at Barry in open curiosity. How could Barry know that he had been thinking of Maine the last few days? Sara would love it; the two of them hadn't had a decent vacation for a year or more. He went to the door. "Maybe I will." He turned the knob.

Barry said, "Let me know about Greg."

Frank nodded and went out.

The battered gray van traveled at an even sixty-five on the secondary road, headlights showing a desolate countryside as the truck twisted and turned on the slight grades. They were in a series of low sand hills, gradually working their way down to a broad valley.

Red looked at his watch. "Snap it up a little, Jake. We're due in forty minutes."

The driver grunted. Red glanced into the back of the van where Scoey was sitting on the floor staring at the canister. Scoey couldn't get used to the idea that there was enough crap in that steel barrel to kill off the population of three states. Maybe more. And besides, the stuff was odorless and invisible. Red grinned in the darkness of the cab. He knew what Scoey was thinking. How did they know the damn gas wasn't leaking out now?

Because they were still alive. Scoey hadn't liked it when Red had said it. "Man, as long as you're still breathing, the thing ain't leaking."

They had timed it to reach the campsite at two in the morning. Red lit a cigarette and tapped the folded map with his finger. He knew that damned map by heart. He could see the road they were traveling now . . . a black line on the paper. In a few minutes they would cross an unused railroad track. Then they'd turn right, go through a burg named Gandy and be home free. There was nothing past Gandy at all. Gandy was the kind of place where everyone went to bed with the chickens. It had a population of about fourteen, including kids.

This section of the country had been chosen for the

getaway partly because the road past Gandy led nowhere. The campsite was at the end of the valley in a collection of trees and rocks. The road stopped. You could get past the campsite on a mule or by walking, but no other way. It was almost straight down a steep mountain for two miles. The military would figure nobody in his right mind would go to all the trouble to steal the canister, then be dumb enough to take it into a cul de sac road. So the search would go elsewhere—at least at first. Long enough for them to make the switch and head east.

It was ten minutes to two when they arrived.

Irene and Turich had a fire going beside the camper. They were drinking beer and listening to the radio.

"Jesus," Red said, climbing out of the cab, "You look like Mom'n Pop Kettle. Anybody around?"

"Hell no," Turich said. He was big and rawboned, with thinning hair and sloping shoulders. "Who the hell'd camp in this damn place? It's a month till fishing's open."

Irene said, "How'd it go?"

"No sweat."

She frowned. "Where's Willy?"

Jake stared at Red. "He bought it from one of the guards. We left 'im out in the sticks."

Irene looked at the two of them. She was short and blonde, washed out and tired looking. She had been picked for those looks.

The stocky Red took charge. "Let's get moving. Back the van around, Jake." He went over to the camper while Jake maneuvered the van. He and Turich removed the back of the camper; it had been designed and built especially for this job. With the back removed, the floor of the van and the floor of the camper were exactly the same height.

It was the work of less than a half hour to roll the heavy canister and rig from the van to the camper. The rig was then dismantled and the canister was enclosed by a thin veneer of sheet metal, bolted on, and jockeyed into position. Scoey and Turich connected dummy pipes. In an hour the canister would pass muster as a water heater if the investigation was not too close. The back of the camper was replaced.

"All right," Red said, "you two get going. When was the ranger here last?"

"Wasn't no ranger," Turich said, "he was a fire warden. He came by two days ago. Irene told him we were leavin' today on our way east. He put the sticker on the windshield."

"He take your names?"

Turich nodded.

Red grinned in satisfaction. "Okay. You'n Irene get going. We'll take care of the rest." He watched them get into the camper and start the engine.

At first light, Red routed them out. Turich had left four motorcycles behind. Red and Scoey muscled one of them into the van. They tossed the remains of the rig in and Jake backed the van out of the trees and down to the road.

The particular spot had been chosen, not only because of the cul de sac, but because of the deep gorges. Eons ago water had eaten the soil away, causing rock falls, and ultimately causing a series of deep narrow gorges that led in tortuous twistings to the valley two miles below. Jake drove the van over a bumpy, rocky field to the edge of the nearest gorge. He halted it twenty feet from the edge and looked at Red.

"What you waiting for?" Red growled. He stood, hands on hips. "Hurry up, I wanta be forty miles from here in another hour."

Jake opened the door of the cab. Releasing the handbrake, he yanked out the throttle and jumped. The van lurched, engine roaring. It reached the edge and

24

went over in a heavy swan dive, wheels spinning.

"Jeez Christ, lookit that thing!" Scoey said in awe.

The van hit the opposite wall of the gorge a hundred feet down and smoke bellowed up. They could hear the shattering crash—then another and another as the wreck came to rest in the jumbled rocks. They could see no fire; the smoke and dust fanned out and in another minute it was still and quiet. Jake whistled, backing away from the edge.

"Let's go," Red said. They went back, brushing out the marks of the van's wheels in the dirt. When Red was satisfied, they got on the bikes and headed into the hills to the south. There were cattle trails there and a few firebreaks. Cyclists could make it to the next highway fifty miles distant.

If they were careful about tracks at the start, no one would ever know they'd been at the campsite at all.

Chapter Three

Barry spent the early morning riding and talking horses. A dealer came up from Harrisburg with four beautiful quarter horses. Barry's stablemaster, Pete Christy, admired three of them exceedingly and finally a deal was made. The dealer went back with money and two horses from Barry's stable and left the three chestnuts.

Later Barry flew to Northrup, a small town on the Susquehanna River, where he examined and made trial spins in several new helicopters which were needed by one of his New England companies. Frank Trask remonstrated with him about wasting time, but Barry loved to fly choppers and could not be talked out of the trip.

He was back at the mansion office shortly after noon and was surprised to find Vera Crawford at her desk.

"What're you doing here? I thought you were in Utah."

She smiled. "I was, boss. Frank sent me out in one of the house planes last night."

Barry sat down opposite her. Vera had her own large airy office next to his. It was tastefully decorated, mostly by her, with landscapes on the walls and rich walnut furniture which contrasted, like a touch of oriental spice, with the maroon hangings and patterned draperies.

He said, "Tell me about it."

"Well, we barely saw Greg. He was in a private room and there was a man present all the time—as though censoring every word."

Barry's brow furrowed. "That's odd." Vera looked tired and her eyes were red-rimmed. She shouldn't be in the office at all. He wondered if Frank Trask knew she was back.

"It was a strange setup, Barry. Greg looked fine, a little pale, but okay. He had a gunshot wound—"

"Gunshot?!"

Vera nodded. "I managed to learn that, but they weren't happy that I had. I think they wanted me to believe it was an ordinary accident." She leaned back and crossed her legs. "But Greg *is* a soldier and accidents *do* happen on the ranges. Greg's told me about a few. So why should they attempt to cover this one up?"

"Because maybe it didn't happen on a rifle range," Barry said promptly. "Where's he stationed?"

"At some Godforsaken little post out in the desert. I don't even know the name, if it's got one."

"What branch is he in?"

"Chemical warfare. He transferred from Ordnance a year ago."

Barry nodded. "Go on."

"That's about it. It took us ten times as long to get in as they allowed us to see him. Greg said he'd have to give Vicky a raincheck on the trip they'd planned. And then they gave us the bum's rush. So we didn't even stay the night. We got right back on the plane and came home."

Chemical warfare . . . Barry showed no surprise. To Vera, he made excuses for the military mind. "You know how cautious they are. Maybe there's a trial coming up or something and Greg isn't allowed to talk about it. Some clown may have fired off a rifle in a messhall."

Vera sniffed. "Greg is an old hand. A thing like that

wouldn't faze him. But he was nervous and shaken up. I can tell—I lived with him long enough. Something important happened, boss."

"But you have no inkling what?"

"Not an idea. They hustled me and Vicky out, escorted us to the plane, and watched us take off." She shrugged. "They were polite as hell, but no questions, ma'am."

Barry smiled and stood. "Well, Greg will tell you all about it eventually. Right now, I want you to knock off. Let one of the other girls take over. You go get some rest."

"But—"

Barry looked severe. "That's an order."

She sighed. "Yes, boss."

In his office Barry called Frank Trask. "Frank, I just talked with Vera."

"I tried to get her to leave, Barry. She's concerned about the San Martin petroleum mix-up."

"That can wait. I told her to go home. This thing piques my curiosity, Frank. Greg is Chem Warfare. Is there a Chemical Warfare operation in that part of Utah?"

Frank was businesslike. "I'll find out and get back to you."

He was back in fifteen minutes. He came in and flopped in one of the easy chairs, fiddling with a pipe. "I tried my highest source, Barry. Some information was easy to get—I think because a year ago there was a television report about the Chemical Warfare depots. They admit there is such a depot and that's about all."

Barry raised his shoulders an inch. "What kind of depot?"

Frank waited a dramatic second. "Nerve gas," he said.

Barry stared at the dumpy man with the pipe, thoughts rushing through his head. Nerve gas was

28

deadly. It was odorless and colorless. There had been a bit of it dropped somewhere in the west by accident and it had wiped out a hell of a lot of sheep. There had also been a lot of speculation about what it would do in a city.

Frank said, "They store nerve gas M-34 GB at a place called Point Archer. That's probably where Greg was. It's in the middle of nowhere." He tamped tobacco into the pipe, looking up owlishly at Barry. "Do we have business with nerve gas?"

Barry shook his head. "Of course not. I told you, it was just curiosity. Vera said Greg was nervous and upset about something. And he had a gunshot wound."

Frank nodded and lit the pipe. "She told me. Let the government worry about this, Barry. It's an internal affair. They can straighten it out without us."

"How d'you know what it is?"

"I don't, really. I guess I'm thinking about that Maine trip."

Barry laughed.

But after Frank had left, he stared at the telephone. It *was* curious. He did have the curiosity of a litter of cats . . . as Frank never ceased telling him. Why cover up something so ordinary as a gunshot wound with all that security?

He picked up the phone and dialed a Washington Pentagon number, asking for Fritz de Bausset. Fritz was his contact man for military matters. Fritz was astonished that he knew about the trouble at Point Archer. Fritz made the mistake Barry hoped for and thought Barry knew more than he did.

"God, that's top-secret stuff, Barry! I mean top!"

"But you admit that someone broke in—"

"I don't admit a damned thing. How'd you find out?"

"A contact." Barry chuckled. "I know you can't talk on the phone. I'm coming down there. I'll call you and we'll have lunch. Right?"

"Sure, Barry. Tomorrow?"

"About one." He hung up and stared at the window. So there was something funny going on. Top secret, too. He had evoked anguished wails by mentioning that someone had broken into the depot. That meant he had hit on the truth. But why would anyone want to steal nerve gas?

He didn't like the feel of it.

It was an uneventful journey. Red, Scoey, and Jake arrived at the town of Cutler at sundown and wheeled the three motorcycles into Pringle's garage. They were more than four hundred miles from Point Archer and had three hundred more to go.

Pringle, a squat, greasy-looking man, was waiting for them. He had been walking impatiently up and down, from the back door to the front, for an hour. "Jesus, it took you long enough——"

"Relax," Red said, slapping dust from his pants. "You got anything to eat here?"

"Jesus, haven't you ate nothing?"

"We been on them goddamn bikes for hours," Scoey said grumpily. "You try it sometime."

Pringle looked out at the road. "Where's the other one, the kid, Willy?"

"He won't be comin'," Red said. "He took one in the ticker. We had to leave him."

"You had trouble? What happened?"

Red shrugged and fished for a crumpled pack, extracting a bent cigarette, straightening it. "The Army seen us when we were making a run for it. We had the tank in the back so we were scootin'. Then Willy got a rush of the braves and started firin' that burp gun." He cupped his hands around a match and held it to the cigarette. "The rest is okay. Irene and Turich are long gone."

Pringle looked at him. They had left a guy. He had a

feeling there was more to it than that but he decided to ask no more questions. No one would be able to trace Willy to them. He glanced at the clock on the wall. "Come on, we're half an hour late getting out of here."

"They're going to have to wait," Red said. He pointed to the sign, Cafe, half a block away. "We'll be back soon's we get fed." He marched out. Scoey and Jake followed.

Pringle smoked a cigarette and swore under his breath. Yashar would raise hell. Yashar liked things to go off like clockwork. Pringle glared at the distant cafe sign. That was what you got for hiring ordinary hoods to do a job for you. They had no goddamn loyalty; eat first, then do the job.

Pringle went into the garage and thumbed through the telephone book where he had written the number. He dialed with the book on his knee. The phone rang five times before someone answered.

"It's Pringle."

The voice said, "Just a sec."

In a moment Pringle heard the familiar heavy voice. "Go on . . ."

"Everything went as planned. They got the package okay. It's on the road in the camper."

"Fine, fine," Yashar sounded pleased.

"One thing . . . Red says they were seen. Willy was killed in the getaway."

"What does it matter?"

Pringle said, "I think it's stupid to take a chance. I've got a contact there. He'll know if anyone saw them. All right?"

"You are right . . . handle it."

Pringle nodded. "All right. We'll be there in about four and a half hours."

"Good," Yashar said, and hung up.

Pringle lit a cigarette and thought about it. Willy didn't matter because he had come from Canada—no one knew him. But Red, Scoey, and Jake had prison records as he had himself. It was possible to connect all of them. And if the FBI connected them, it might be possible to connect Yashar into it too. Yashar wouldn't like that.

He had the Olds parked in front of the garage when they returned. The three others climbed in and Pringle put the car in gear. It would take a long time to cover the three hundred. They'd get there at midnight or a little after.

Yashar had picked a spot about midway between Point Archer and Medwick, where the second canister had been obtained. The plan was to bury the canister in a field. Yashar and one other man would be there waiting for them—and it should have been the other way round. Pringle and the three men were supposed to arrive first and have the hole dug.

Red and the others caved in as soon as the Olds was on the highway. Pringle was annoyed. At least he had expected company. Red and Jake were in the back, Scoey in the front seat. And all of them went to sleep, with Jake snoring.

Pringle sighed deeply. Well, the sonsofbitches would have no excuse about being tired when they arrived. They could dig the hole without bitching.

Kel Grodin was a tall, rangy redhead, a man who could fly a surfboard if someone would put a prop on it. He picked Barry up in the middle of the morning and drove him to the strip. The Hewes-Bradford complex, Hewesridge, topped a low mountain; the flying strip was at the foot, a four mile journey through pine forests.

There were two hangars, one empty, the other containing the Star Jet and a small cabin prop plane. The mechanics had the plane warmed and ready. Barry climbed in and Kel had the jet in the air in another few minutes.

They were in Washington D.C. fifteen minutes before noon. Barry called Fritz de Bausset from the airport, got a cab to the Dominique and engaged a small private dining room. He had time for a martini before Fritz arrived.

Fritz was a short, bushy-haired man of fifty-six; he had a round, pleasant face and a computer mind. The maître' d ushered him into the room and Fritz made a face as the door closed.

"Dammit, Barry, I've never been in here before. Not even with the way the generals spend dough!" He looked around admiringly. The room was peach, with a glittering chandelier and an antique sideboard. He seated himself, leaning across for a quick handshake. "What're you buttering me up for?"

Barry laughed. "Curiosity. Have a drink."

"Why not?" Fritz rubbed his stubby hands together. "Make it a scotch and water."

Barry clicked the intercom and ordered the drink sent in. He leaned back. "To get to the point, I'm interested in nerve gas." He watched the expression on Fritz' face. The short man looked grim, then puzzled, then he sighed, all in the space of a second or two.

"I don't know where the hell you get your information, Barry." He pursed his lips and opened his mouth again—and there was a knock at the door. Fritz said nothing as the waiter came in with the drink, placed it deftly in front of Fritz, and went out, all in one fluid motion.

"Some friends of mine were hurt by what happened," Barry said. He sipped the martini. "Is this going to make international waves?"

Fritz took a breath. He gulped the scotch and put the glass down. "Probably. We don't know yet what the hell it means." He fixed Barry with a narrowed eye. "This goes no further, of course." At Barry's nod he continued. "Yes, a canister of M-34 GB was stolen from

33

Point Archer. There *was* a firefight. One of our men was killed and four wounded by bullets. We killed one of them, or damn near."

"What d'you mean?"

Fritz shrugged. "We found a body. The man had been badly shot up by rifle fire, then killed by a pistol bullet fired at close range. They knocked him off rather than take him along."

"Pretty cold blooded."

"Very." Fritz nodded. "That gives you an idea of the kind of people we're up against. Your friend Greg Crawford was one of those wounded."

Barry smiled. Fritz had done some investigating and learned about Greg.

"That isn't all," Fritz said. "There was an unlucky shot fired. It unsealed a canister and gas leaked. Seven more dead and five may die." He gulped the rest of the scotch and rattled the ice in the glass. "A nasty business."

"No leads on the canister?"

Fritz frowned. "I haven't told you the worst yet."

Barry waited, eyes on the other.

"Point Archer wasn't the only depot hit that same night." Fritz punctuated his next remark by rapping the glass on the table. "They also hit four other depots and got away with four more canisters!"

Barry caught his breath. "Five canisters of nerve gas?!"

"Right. Enough to wipe out God knows how many people . . . maybe the entire goddamn United States!"

Barry slumped in the chair. This was more than he had expected. Such an operation had to be planned with split-second timing and had cost a great deal of money. With five canisters of that kind of deadly poison, a man or a group could blackmail the world. Barry's concern showed on his face.

Fritz nodded. "It's got everybody who knows about it

so jumpy they can't sit still. A major had a heart attack this morning during high-level briefing. The President himself came to see the pictures. We've got a complete set of pictures of each depot after the raid. Mostly the raiders hit and run, depended on speed . . ."

"But the body. Have you found out who it is?"

The short man shrugged. "It hasn't helped. He was a small-time strong-arm type, obviously hired for the job. It's led us nowhere, for the time being. We're looking for his friends and contacts now. We may turn up something. But that's not the main problem."

"Yes," Barry said. "Why did they steal the canisters."

Fritz nodded. "Blackmail diplomacy. It has to be that. So far we've had no contact from them. We don't even know who 'they' are."

"Or where they've hidden the gas."

"Right," Fritz sighed. "The thing was planned so well that the canisters disappeared into thin air."

Barry frowned. Where do you conceal five large and heavy steel canisters? They could be temporarily buried in some out of the way place, of course. Maybe that's what had happened. Maybe each one had been lowered into a prepared hole in the ground. Then, when the demands of the thieves were made and met, the government would be told where to dig them up.

Maybe. And maybe not.

No wonder Greg Crawford had been nervous and upset. No wonder the security had been suddenly airtight. If this kind of story got out, if people were told that the entire countryside could be flooded with invisible, odorless poison gas, what kinds of riots and panic would ensue?

Fritz sighed deeply. "And all we can do is wait," he said. "Whoever has the gas is in the driver's seat."

They left the restaurant separately, at Fritz' request.

Barry paused in the bar, exchanging greetings with several acquaintances, listening to Washington gossip. He was curious to discover if the Point Archer affair had leaked out. But no one mentioned it.

As he approached the foyer looking for a telephone, a woman touched his arm. "Barry! How nice to see you."

It was Eunice Fontaine, wife of Lieutenant General Harry Fontaine, one of the big guns at the Pentagon. He took her hand. "Eunice, what a surprise!"

"I didn't know you were in town, Barry."

"I'm not, really. I just came in for a quick appointment."

Eunice drew him aside out of the press of diners hurrying past them in groups. "You're just the man I want to see. We're having a few people in this evening, Barry. You must come! I won't take no for an answer."

Barry hesitated. He had been planning on returning to Pennsylvania immediately but Harry Fontaine *was* a gun at the center of military operations. And Harry was prone to talk with a few drinks in him. Harry wasn't stupid but he did tend to brag and talk big to the right people. Barry was one of those people. You never could tell, maybe he'd learn something.

"I'd be delighted, Eunice," he said. He kissed her hand quickly. "Expect me."

"Wonderful, Barry." She squeezed his fingers and flew away.

Barry found the telephone and called the airfield. Kel Grodin was happy to stay overnight. He knew a girl in town, he said.

Frank Trask grumped a bit. "You should take Lobo along, Barry. Those Washington parties are being attended by riff-raff these days . . ."

Chapter Four

Ali Yashar was a big man. He was swarthy, with a shock of black hair, a thick moustache, and eyes that glowed like coals when he was angry. He was angry now. Pringle and the men were overdue.

They had no way to telephone. There was only one thing to do. Wait. He got out of the truck, growling something to Benny, slamming the door, and walked. It was a dark night, with only a sliver of pale moon. They were fifteen miles from the nearest habitation, on a dirt road, in the middle of nowhere. He considered the possibility that Pringle had gotten lost—but no, Pringle knew this country too well.

He went back to the road and found the stake he and Pringle had driven into the earth together—when they had selected the spot. The stake was still there; he kicked it viciously with his foot. This was the spot.

He stood for a long moment listening to the crickets, staring in the direction of the truck. He could barely see it in among the trees. Then Benny lit a cigarette. The match glowed dully in the truck window for a second. Yashar turned away and walked along the lonely road.

Everything had gone well, except for the trouble Pringle reported. All five canisters had been removed from the depots as planned. Two were well on the way to the secret places in Pennsylvania. The other three would be buried. He and Benny had come to this spot with the one from Medwick. The team that had stolen it had been disposed of. The fewer people who knew where the canisters were, the better. Benny and Pringle were his own men, patriots from the movement. He had perhaps twenty men he could trust. The others were nothing.

It was an hour before he saw the distant headlights.

He went quickly back to the truck and alerted Benny. Benny jumped to the ground with a semiautomatic rifle and they hid themselves in the trees.

It was Pringle. The headlights clicked off and on, giving the signal. The Olds pulled into the field and stopped, the engine cut.

"We had to go slow," Pringle reported. "We had to detour some roadblocks."

"All right," Yashar said. "Benny, help them get the package out of the truck."

They put down steel rails and, using the Olds for power, slowly inched the heavy canister out of the truck and eased it to the ground. Pringle got shovels from the trunk of the Olds, and Red and his men set to work. They dug a five-foot deep hole next to the canister, with a sloping side so the thing would roll down.

It took more than an hour. Benny had brought along a bottle and passed it around.

Yashar did not approve of the drinking. While they dug the hole he walked back to the road and paced along it, thinking. He would go east now and prepare the next step in the plan. Soon he would be ready to move.

When he heard the yell, he paused and stared toward the lanterns Benny had set up so they could see to dig. Yashar saw at a glance they had rolled the canister into the hole and were shoveling dirt over it. The breeze carried the dust off to the right.

One of the men was on his knees and a second was running from the site. Benny yelled, then ran to the truck. Pringle was already behind the wheel and the engine roared into life. The truck bumped across the field toward Yashar. Near the hole, the running man stumbled and dropped to the ground. Yashar's heart was hammering in his chest.

The canister had ruptured!

Benny shouted at him and Yashar grabbed at the door as the truck slowed. He jumped into the cab as Pringle raced the engine, heading down the road at breakneck speed.

"They're dead!" Benny shouted. "Jake keeled right on top of the goddamn hole, then Red. Scoey tried to run—!"

"What the hell happened?" Yashar shook the hysterical man.

"I dunno. They rolled it into the hole. Just about had it covered when Jake started to choke. He sort of jerked—then—Jeez!"

Yashar glanced back. The slight breeze undoubtedly had saved Benny and Pringle and himself. The gas had been carried away from them.

Benny swore and wiped his hand over his sweating face. "Sooner or later someone's gonna spot the car and bodies . . ."

Yashar growled to himself. First the trouble at Point Archer, now this. Pringle and his men had botched it. Fools. But it would make no difference if one canister was found. It would change nothing.

The plan would be carried out.

Camp Grafton was sixty-eight miles from Point Archer, more or less, as the crow flies. It was a small post that had once been used as an infantry training ground but was now largely deactivated. The huge military reservation was ringed with fence, patrolled once a day. Occasionally hunters or campers invaded the quiet of the desert and now and then a wandering prospector snooped through.

Grafton's military population was somewhat less than two thousand; there were several training schools and ranges and a small hospital at the edge of the town, which was also called Grafton.

The military hospital was a sprawling structure, a series of radiating arms, all one story. The hospital currently used only two of the corridors for patients. Sergeant Greg Crawford was in one of these, with two MP's as guards at all times. Sergeant Crawford was considered a valuable witness should the investigation turn up any of the men who might have been involved in the raid on the Point Archer Depot.

He was the only man who had actually seen any of the raiders.

A man whom Crawford recognized came into the room with the doctor who was making his rounds. Major Birney smiled and came over to the bed. "How are you, Sergeant?"

"Fine, sir. Did you come to get me out of this place?"

Birney glanced at the doctor. "Matter of fact I did. If the doctor here says you can go."

The doctor smiled. He was young and very pale in contrast to the Major who was deeply tanned. "The wound isn't going to be fatal."

Major Birney said, "We want you to come back to Point Archer, Sergeant. We've got an investigatory team there and it will save time if you're on hand when they want you. Think you can make the trip?"

"Hell yes, Major." Crawford struggled up on his elbows. "This room is driving me nuts."

The doctor left them and Birney sat on the edge of the bed. "We'll take you over in an ambulance. I hear you got it in the chest."

Crawford looked down at the bandages, nodding. "A nice clean one, sir, they tell me. Missed the lung."

"You were lucky." Birney lit a cigarette. "Sorry, you can't have one of these. There'll be some high brass in

40

on the questioning. We're hoping you can put us onto the bad guys."

"I got a good look at one of them, sir, and the truck they were using."

Birney got up. "Good. Get all the rest you can. The ambulance will call for you after dark." He went out with a casual wave.

After supper they brought Greg socks and shoes, put him in a wheelchair, and took him outside to the car. It was not a regular ambulance but a car with reclining seats. Crawford was able to sit up. They put him in the seat with a blanket over him, a corpsman slid under the wheel, and they took off. Another car with four MPs led the way.

The driver said, "Hi, sarge, you're getting the VIP treatment."

"The hell I am. They should have taken me in a chopper."

"The generals like the choppers for themselves. Besides I think there's only one around here. The Air Force has it over at the field." He settled himself in the seat. "They call me Gabby. What's your name?"

"Greg Crawford. You got any cigarettes?"

"You're not s'posed to have any, they told me."

"I didn't ask you that."

Gabby shrugged and passed over a pack. "Okay, so you pulled rank on me."

They followed the MP car out of town and headed southeast on a lonely highway. No one expected trouble, Greg knew, or they wouldn't have sent him like this. He was an important witness, so the cover of dark and the car full of MPs was routine.

They met a few cars at widely spaced intervals but none passed them. It was a monotonous journey over a mostly flat landscape. He could see little beyond the window glass but the strip of asphalt in the headlights and the back of the car ahead of them. A barbed wire

41

fence to their right marched for miles bordering the road.

Twenty miles after leaving Grafton they came to a series of roller-coaster dips. The dips, a hundred feet from crest to crest, were probably formed by washes, Crawford thought, run-off from the hills. After the third one, the road turned to the right in a gentle curve then straightened out.

Gabby said, "Dry lake off over there."

"You make this trip often?"

"Maybe once a month. We take turns mannin' the infirmary over at Point Archer." Gabby glanced at him. "Guess I never seen you there."

"I don't go on sick call much."

"Guess not."

The dry lake ended and they began to climb a slope. There were a few trees; the road twisted now and then.

Greg fiddled with the car radio, getting nothing but static. He felt restless. For a time he tried to interest Gabby in talking and was surprised when the other did not respond. For all his name, Gabby was strangely untalkative.

Then he noticed that Gabby was glancing into the rear view mirror constantly, as if expecting to see something there.

Greg eased himself in the seat, turning sideways. His chest hurt and he rested, then turned again.

There was a car following them! Without lights. He stared at it, astonished. It looked like a pickup, coming like hell. He said, "Hey—there's a car!"

"A car?" Gabby said, a little lamely. He stared at the rear view.

Greg reached over and pounded the horn ring.

Gabby looked startled, then he knocked Greg's hand away. "Cut it out! Whatchoo trying to do?"

"There's a car behind us," Greg said loudly. He saw the brake light flare in the MP car. A blur of white face in the rear window; he stuck his arm out and waved.

"It's just a car," Gabby said. "What the hell, some guy driving without lights."

The pickup truck was alongside them in another second without slackening speed. Greg Crawford stared into the gun muzzle flashes, realizing that he was seeing and hearing the chatter of a submachine gun. He felt Gabby slam on the brakes.

Bullets pounded the side of the car, shattering the side window and the windshield. Greg ducked, yelling. He heard Gabby screaming, yelling something at the other car.

"It's me—Gabby!"

The pickup passed them. Greg was rigid, hands gripping the seat. The shock of it immobilized him. He stared at Gabby. The man was cut and bleeding but alive. Gabby was sawing the car back and forth across the road, slowing down rapidly, skidding in the sand.

"Cut the lights," Greg yelled. "Get outa here—go back the other way!"

Gabby was swearing steadily, fighting the wheel, trying to get the car turned.

· There were shots from the MP car, and the stutter of submachine guns answered. Greg jerked his head around. The MP car had run off the road into the brush and trees. He could see the pickup truck slowing, brake lights flaring red.

"They're coming back!" he yelled.

Gabby continued to swear. He had the car straightened out, heading back toward Grafton. He was giving it the gas, but it sputtered and jerked. The engine had been hit. Greg saw the irregular line of jagged holes along the side of the hood; some of the bullets had ripped long ragged grooves across it.

The pickup's lights flashed on, very bright.

Gabby leaned out, waving his arm. "It's Gabby!" he yelled. "It's me!"

Greg stared at the man. Gabby *knew* the attackers and he was trying to save his own neck! Greg made a grab for him but Gabby shoved him away.

Gabby screamed, "They're after *you*, dammit!"

Greg had no chance to reply. The rear window shattered. The car was suddenly full of flying lead and debris. Crawford felt a slug rip through his shoulder. He heard the stutter of the guns and felt the car swerve. There was nothing at all he could do. Gabby's hands dropped from the wheel as another burst of fire caught him and he fell forward. The car bumped hard as it left the asphalt. It slammed into a dirt bank and toppled on its side. The guns were still firing.

That was the last sound Greg heard.

Chapter Five

The Fontaine apartment was large, in the fashionable Georgetown section of Washington. Barry arrived in a rented Cadillac, pondering the news that General Fontaine had been called out of town. This information had come to him only moments before - he had gone downstairs to get into the chauffeured limo.

Most of the guests had already arrived; Barry knew all of them, albeit some very slightly, and made the rounds shaking hands and kissing some of the women. Eunice Fontaine took his arm in a rather aggressive manner as if proud to parade her latest social catch. The apartment reflected the military caste of its owner. It was almost ostentatious; the den displayed trophies garnered in far parts of the world and there were antiques on the walls and in the corners of every room.

Eunice was Fontaine's second wife, Barry knew, a much younger woman. He thought she might be thirty-four or five. General Fontaine was probably twice that and Washington rumors held that Eunice was less than faithful . . . but *very* discreet. She said, "I'm so annoyed that Harry had to go off somewhere today—"

Barry smiled. "You'll manage. Was it business or did he go fishing?" He was fishing himself.

"Business. He had to go to Utah, of all places. How long are you staying in Washington, darling?"

"I have to get back tomorrow."

"Back to where? Barry, you do get around more than any man I know. Last week you were in—where was it? Afghanistan?"

He laughed. "Iceland. I only flew in and out. How did you know?"

"It was in the paper." Eunice shrugged. "You're news, Barry darling. Someone found out you were there."

"I'll wear my false moustache next time." He said it lightly but it sometimes annoyed him that his movements were so meticulously reported when reporters could trace him. He usually took more than careful pains to assure privacy; he never allowed pictures to be taken of him, and he avoided places where an enterprising cameraman might snap one without his knowledge. Too often it was inhibiting to whatever business he was engaged in to be announced in the press; worse, the press apparently loved to speculate on his business and almost always distorted the facts because they had too few on which to theorize.

Dinner was almost formal, a long table in the yellow dining room; the walls were a Parisian print, the draperies butter yellow relieved with flecks of white. A huge chandelier hung over them. Barry was placed at Eunice's right, across from Senator Lesberg, one of the wheels of the Military Affairs Committee. A young redhead, wife of an attaché, sat on Barry's right, chattering about England. She was delighted with London, its atmosphere and pomp. Barry almost missed the signal which brought Lesberg out of his chair.

He glanced at Eunice and her lips formed the words, "The telephone."

When Lesberg returned to his place, he seemed preoccupied.

The wife of a State Department official, a middle-aged matron with a petulant voice, was decrying the worsening relations between the United States and Kushka, a Persian Gulf state. Barry heard her with half an ear, then noticed Senator Lesberg's eyebrows raise a half inch. Lesberg seemed very annoyed by her chatter and Barry wondered why.

He was slightly surprised to hear nothing at all—not a word of gossip—about the stolen gas canisters. The secret must be very well kept. An unusual circumstance in Washington.

Over brandy, Eunice curled a finger into his and insisted he pay more attention to her. "A girl can get jealous, you know."

Barry was accustomed to the sometimes not-so-subtle hints of women. Eunice was possibly the most attractive female in the room—probably the other guests had been invited partly on the basis of looks. Why invite competition if you're intending to seduce one particular and very interesting man? Someone had once said that to him, in just those words.

He wondered if Eunice knew of the canister raids.

It was difficult to pursue any vein of thought with everyone bent on making conversation. He gave it up for the time being. Senator Lesberg made his apologies shortly after dinner and went out to his car with a protesting wife. Barry watched them go. Were there sudden developments about the nerve gas that demanded Lesberg's attention?

When Barry could slip away he called Fritz de Bausset from a bedroom phone, intending to ask for the latest news. But Fritz was not at home.

Later, Barry accompanied Eunice to her bedroom. They had never been intimate before and he was somewhat amused at her casual approach. She undressed quickly, then helped him off with his shoes. "I've often wondered what you'd look like naked."

He said, "I hope it's not a disappointment."

"Oh God no, Barry! You should—" She stopped suddenly and he wondered exactly what she had been about to say. Then she came into his arms eagerly.

They made love and he found her less than casual, overeager, in fact. She would not stay satisfied.

Then they lit cigarettes. Eunice had brought a bottle to the bedside and they had a bit of vintage cognac that glinted like gold in the glasses. Barry asked, "Why Utah?"

"What?"

"Why did Harry go to Utah?"

"Oh, there was a shooting or something. He didn't tell me much. I can't imagine why they'd want Harry for a mere shooting, can you?"

"There must be more to it than that. Maybe a poker party?"

Eunice giggled. "You think he really went to Vegas? Maybe he did, the old sonofabitch." She blinked at him. "No, he went in uniform and he didn't take civies at all."

"And he left in a hurry?"

"God yes. Like a shot." She looked at him lazily, under long, black lashes. "D'you know what's up, Barry?"

He shook his head. "I'm innocent."

"I'll bet you are. You probably know twice as much as the fat cats in the State Department. The last time Harry took off like that we got into a war. He was gone for six months—and he only had two stars then."

"It's not a war," Barry said with confidence.

"But you do know what it is?"

Barry sighed. "I'm beginning to get a very good idea."

He left the Fontaine apartment at three in the morning and drove to the Carillon Hotel where Hewes-Bradford maintained rooms on a year-round basis. He was undressing, again, when the phone rang. A clerk wanted to know if Mr. Hewes-Bradford would accept a call from a Mr. Whitehead.

"Yes, of course," Barry said. Whitehead was the code-name for Fritz de Bausset.

"Barry," Fritz said, "we've got info on the dead man I told you about. His name and those of a half dozen friends. Some of them are missing from regular haunts. I thought you'd like to know."

"What kind of people?"

"The lowest forms. No political connections."

48

"Hired for the job then?"

"Strictly," Fritz said. "Nothing more."

"Is there a high-level conference in Utah?"

Fritz paused a second. "Yes. Called only tonight—I mean last night. The highest." He chuckled. "Am I telling you anything you don't know?"

"Just checking."

Fritz sighed. "Sometimes I think you know more than I do, even when it happens in my lap." He rang off.

In the morning Barry called Trask and asked him to have Lobo standing by with a car. He and Kel Grodin should arrive at the Hewesridge strip by ten o'clock.

They had a tail wind and Grodin made good time. The Star Jet touched down at the Hewes-Bradford strip at nine-forty-five. Lobo was waiting. And he had news.

"Bad news, Barry," he said when Barry got in the car. "Greg Crawford is dead."

"He died of his wounds?"

"Worse than that. He was being taken somewhere by the military for questioning and his car was ambushed."

"Ambushed?!" Barry sat up.

Lobo nodded. "They didn't tell us much. Frank called back after someone called to notify Vera. He got hold of some general or other and was able to wring a few words out. Greg's car was ambushed and he and the driver were shot to death. The escort car of MP's bought it, too."

Barry stared through the windshield, seeing nothing. This was definitely a wide-scale plan if they had taken the trouble to go back and eliminate a possible witness. And Greg had been killed under the noses of the military.

Lobo said, "Does it change things?" Lobo was a husky man with straw-colored hair. His name was Lloyd Fenner but very few called him Lloyd since he had gained the nickname Lobo on the football field. He put the car in gear and started up the hill toward Hewesridge.

"I'm afraid it does. My hunch is that all hell is going to break loose very soon. Any group with the moxie to steal five canisters of nerve gas, one of the most deadly weapons ever devised, has plans to use it."

"How?"

"Blackmail, probably," Barry said. "On a national scale." He was silent a moment. Lobo tooled the car up the winding road, frowning through the windshield.

"Pretty cool stuff, killing the only possible witness that way."

"Yes, but it means they know they can be stopped. Otherwise they wouldn't bother. How'd you like to go to Utah?"

Lobo shrugged and grinned. "When do I leave?"

"We'll talk with Frank first."

The talk was held in Barry's hexagonal office but postponed an hour at Frank Trask's request. When he came in, Frank had a sheaf of papers in his hand, his unlit pipe in his mouth. He sat down in a chair facing Barry, brushed ashes off his thighs, nodded to Lobo, and said he was sorry he'd taken so much time.

"But I've got some info I think you'll want."

Barry said, "Let's put everything else aside for the moment and concentrate on the stolen gas canister problem."

Frank nodded, "That's what I've done." He looked at Barry, who smiled.

Lobo said, "It would do my ego good if you'd make a mistake now and then, Frank."

"Negative," Frank said. "Can't afford mistakes." He scratched his nearly bald head. "The question is: who'd want to steal five canisters of deadly nerve gas, right?"

"Very close," Barry said gravely. Frank Trask sometimes astonished him, even though he'd known the stocky little man for years. Frank had the ability to an-

50

ticipate. He tried to think back . . . what had he said to Frank to cause the man to go into the canister thing immediately? The trip to Washington? He had looked into other Hewes-Bradford business while in town. He said, "Go on, Frank, you've got the floor."

"All right." Frank smiled at both of them and patted the papers. "I asked myself that question right off. Who'd want to steal the stuff and why. I've come up with several possibilities and a couple of reasons. Except that I tend toward one very strongly."

"Blackmail," Barry said and Frank nodded.

"But let's take the groups first. This is obviously a well-organized bunch—look at how widely spaced the raids were and all carried out the same night. That also means money. They were well financed. Had to be. The first thing I thought of was a political action bunch calling itself Patriots for Freedom."

Lobo said, "I've seen items about them in the papers."

"Right. They've been causing riots and various other kinds of trouble coast to coast for half a year now." Frank puffed on the unlit pipe, took it out of his mouth, and put it beside him on a coffee table. "The second is organized crime. They probably could handle it. There's the Tarrago Islands, you know. Gangland took them over more than a year ago and no one's done a damn thing about it."

"The Islands don't belong to this country," Barry said.

Frank nodded. "But they do practically all their business with American tourists. Anyway, it proves that organized crime is capable. The third possibility is a group calling itself the International Peace Movement, which is a damned ambiguous title if I ever heard one. According to the papers they've been threatening to make their voices heard. And I have private info that they're well financed and equipped with a flock of zealots—built-in troublemakers. The fourth group I looked at is known as the National Liberation Army of Kushka, a foreign bunch with plenty of ties to the U.S.A."

"You've been busy," Barry said admiringly.

"There's been a lot about the National Liberation Army of Kushka in the papers," Lobo said. "They've been sounding off about some prisoners being held in this country. The CIA intercepted a bomb plot against some top U.S. officials and the would-be Kushka bombers were captured."

Frank Trask nodded. "Exactly. And it fits the possible blackmail theory." He patted the papers he had brought. "The National Liberation Army claims the men are political prisoners and demand their release."

Barry recalled the gossip at Eunice Fontaine's party. Someone had mentioned Kushka and the growing trouble. Hewes-Bradford would be vitally interested in any such trouble because it had extensive oil holdings in Kushka and H-B ships brought oil to the United States. He had been reading a report written by the H-B manager-on-the-spot only this morning about the possibility of trouble. The Shah, a British educated sheik, apparently sided with the NLA militants arguing there was no actual evidence that the NLA had been behind the plot. He wanted the men released and returned to their native country to face trial there. If they were criminals they would be dealt with.

"The Shah is an enlightened man," Frank said, "but he is so insulated from the actual world that facts can easily be kept from him. The NLA may be feeding him selected information. There is a branch of the National Liberation Army here in the U.S. Its leader is a very intelligent radical named Ali Yashar. I haven't been able to find out much about Yashar but I have men digging."

Barry said, "Do you advise going all out in an investigation of the NLA?"

"I think we should look at *all* possibilities, Barry. Remember, we only just got into this. We have a little more info on the NLA because we're concerned with Kushkan oil, but it's possible the NLA may not be behind the nerve gas thefts at all."

"All right." Barry nodded. "That's your department. Let's get information on the other three prospects."

Frank said, "There's a high level investigation going on right now. The military is considerably worked up about the raids—"

"There's been nothing in the papers."

"No, not yet." Trask frowned and fiddled with the pipe. "But it can't be kept secret long. Too many people know about the thefts already. A sensational disclosure would shake up the entire country. There'd be riots and panic for sure."

"What I don't understand," Lobo said, "is why there hasn't been some kind of demand, if we're right that the gas was stolen to be used as blackmail."

Frank grunted. "True. I've been wondering that myself."

"They're not ready," Barry said. "Besides, the conditions are not yet right."

Lobo said, "What d'you mean?"

"Put yourself in their place. If you'd stolen the canisters and wanted some huge concession from the U.S., wouldn't you want the people of the country to be scared to death so they'd clamor for the government to give in to the blackmail?"

Frank and Lobo glanced at each other. "Jesus," Frank said, "if that's true these people think big!" He put the pipe in his mouth and sucked on it. "Hell yes."

Lobo said, "How do you tell a nation it's in danger of being wiped out?"

Chapter Six

A high level conference was held in Washington, chaired by the President's top advisor, Dr. Jack Kittridge. The reports from the five investigatory teams at the raided depots were read. Inferences were drawn and a considerable number of guesses made. It was decided not to bring in the press at this juncture. Investigations were still going on in several different directions and it was hoped that progress would quickly be made.

The search for the canisters had expanded; ground, sea, and air units were at work, covering every inch of territory around each of the five depots. Information had been given to local newsmen that dangerous military prisoners had escaped and the search was on that account. This cover story had been picked up by international news services, but not featured widely.

Then the Gilmer story broke.

POISON DEATHS NEAR GILMER

Three unidentified men were found dead this morning near Gilmer, a farming community twenty miles from Hotchkiss, the country seat.
Sheriff T.R. Belding states that the men apparently died in convulsions. "They must have eaten agricultural poison."
The men were found by Jediah Hosmer, a farmer living nearby. Hosmer, who saw the automobile

parked in a field, said he thought at first the car belonged to hunters.

An investigation into the deaths is continuing.

Sheriff Ted Belding, short, portly, and graying, leaned against his black and white, talking with Deputy John Uchitel. They were watching the Strehl brothers back their wrecker into the field, preparing to haul the Olds to town.

"Think they was burying something?" Uchitel asked, picking his teeth with a little finger. "They's three shovels and a couple of lanterns out there. Soft dirt behind the car, looks like someone's been digging."

"Can't figger it at all. They ain't from around here. Plates on the Olds oughta tell us something." Belding grunted, pushing himself away from the car. He took a few steps along the road, regarding the wheel marks in the earth. It looked like two cars had been here, but maybe not. They'd have to compare tire tracks to find out for sure if it became important. He made a mental note to have Hoss come out and photograph the tracks, just in case. They'd have to go over to Jed Hosmer's place, too, to see if he had driven into the field. Some of the tracks might be his.

He looked around as Uchitel shouted, "Hey—what the hell!"

Uchitel was pointing into the field. Belding stared. The wrecker had halted and Bert Strehl, who had been guiding the truck into position, was now on the ground, kicking and jerking in convulsions. Carl jumped out of the truck and bent over his brother.

Uchitel started into the field. Belding called, "Johnny!"

The deputy paused, looked around.

Belding ran toward him. "Stay outa there!"

"But somethin's happened to Bert!"

Belding pointed. "Get the hell in the car." He ran

55

around to the other side and jerked the door open. "Johnny! Get in the goddamn car!"

Uchitel hesitated and Belding called again. Carl had dropped to his knees and was shaking and trying to wave to them with agonized gestures. In another moment he too sprawled, kicking and jerking on the ground.

Sheriff Belding slid under the wheel of the black and white. The engine roared into life. He backed the car, wheels spinning. Uchitel ran toward it and Belding slowed long enough for the big deputy to fling open the door and throw himself inside. The car took off along the dirt road at high speed. Whatever had killed the three strangers had got Bert and Carl!

Lobo brought the wire services item to Barry. "It came over the radio ten minutes ago. TV and the papers'll have it tonight."

Barry read the item, frowning. Two brothers, Carl and Bert Strehl, had died mysteriously in a lonely field—the same field where three bodies had been discovered only hours before. Cause of death was unknown but had been preceded by violent convulsions.

"Convulsions," Barry said. "That would suggest nerve gas."

Lobo shrugged. "They found shovels in the field. It could be where one of the nerve gas canisters is buried."

Barry nodded. "Put a man on it."

Turich and Irene took Route 70 out of Denver and followed it through Kansas City, St. Louis, Indianapolis, and Pittsburgh. They made good time in the camper, driving by turns and sleeping in the back. They bought food along the way, instead of pausing for meals, and they were never stopped at all for questioning.

Turich pulled off the road twice to change plates.

North of Pittsburgh he put on Pennsylvania plates.

They went farther north, then east again. Turich halted along a country road in daylight and unscrewed a panel in the back of the camper, extracting a sheet of tracing paper. He carefully placed this overlay on an ordinary gas-station map of the state, lining it up with penciled crosses.

Turich tapped the spot marked with an *X* in a circle. " 'Bout a three hour ride I'd say," he remarked, as Irene lit a cigarette. "Half hour out of Thayer."

Thayer was a town of less than five thousand nestled in the hills. They passed through it without stopping, took a side road eleven miles farther, and wound through the hills in the fading light. The road forked; they took the left, a double track with weeds in the center. Five minutes later a new barbed wire fence and gate barred the way.

Turich stopped the car and gave two quick toots on the horn, then two more, then one. Two men stepped from the surrounding trees. Both were armed with submachine guns. One waved, went to the gate, and unlocked it. Turich drove the camper through and kept going.

"We made it, honey," he said to Irene.

"Jesus, I wish I had a bath." She stretched. "How long d'we have to stay here?"

"It ain't up to me." Turich pulled up as another man stepped into the road and pointed. He turned left again and came up against a sheer wall.

He killed the engine and opened the door. Ali Yashar came out of the darkness, his swarthy features wreathed in smiles.

Fritz de Bausset called Barry in the afternoon. "Did you hear about the Gilmer thing?"

"Yes. Is there an upshot?"

"A nerve gas canister was buried in that field. Chem

War sent men in. The thing was leaking. They neutralized the area and dug it up. Your theory was right after all."

"What theory?" Barry asked.

"You said the canisters might be buried somewhere close by the depots where they were stolen."

"Gilmer is nowhere near . . ."

"Listen, I'm giving you the benefit of being right, huh?" Fritz chuckled. "The Joint Chiefs didn't do any better." He paused. "Are you getting into this thing, Barry?"

"I'll do anything I can to help. This situation is too explosive to ignore."

"Do you have any leads on who may be behind it?"

"Not yet. What about the car that was found there?"

"It was registered to a guy in Cutler, that's a small burg. Guy's name is Terrance Pringle. He owns a garage. So far no one's caught up with Pringle."

Barry made a decision. He would go to Washington; the facts were homing there. Hewesridge was too far off the beaten track for this problem. The government investigators would monopolize the field too. Barry's own men would hardly have a chance. The government had the manpower and resources to seal off an entire area till its men raked it over.

"I'm coming back to Washington," he told Fritz. "I'll be at the Carillon but don't mention it around. Call me day or night."

"Right," Fritz said and hung up.

Barry called Kel Grodin and told him to warm up the plane; then he went to see Frank Trask, asking Vera to send Lobo in.

Frank was dead against the Washington trip. "That's the first goddamn place they'll hit with the nerve gas!"

"They won't hit anything until they make demands and get an answer."

Lobo arrived on the run, hearing the last few words.

"Has a demand been made?"

Barry filled him in and Lobo left immediately to pack a bag and to tell Holden to pack one for Barry. For an hour Barry went over foreign communications and current business with Frank and Bert Allard, Frank's assistant. Allard, a tall, graying man of few words, made notes in shorthand. There were no major decisions; a few scheduled meetings could be postponed; Barry would take along a case full of papers to mull over in Washington. There were some aspects of the worldwide Hewes-Bradford empire that had to have his attention. Linard Mariani, in Honolulu, for instance, required his personal okay on a number of important matters.

Lobo drove the car down the mountain to the strip and they were airborne quickly.

Fritz de Bausset was not Barry's only contact in Washington. Fritz was exceptionally well situated for certain kinds of information and Fritz was close-mouthed. Fritz knew of Barry's dedication to peace and over the years had provided valuable assistance in that regard.

Phillip Vosberg, on the other hand, was a man interested in money. He would supply information for a price. Barry had always dealt with Vosberg at arm's length, paying the man his fees and always cloaking requests in business reasons. He called Vosberg on arriving at the Carillon, explaining that he was interested in information regarding Kushka; Vosberg knew of the Hewes-Bradford oil interests in that part of the world. Vosberg promised to keep his ears flapping.

Lobo had his own sources also. He went out, making the rounds, dropping hints, promising money or favors, asking for information on all the prospects mentioned by Frank Trask: organized crime; the International Peace group; the Patriots for Freedom, and the National Liberation Army of Kushka.

Seeing Lobo, a number of people were aware that

Barry was in town. He received a call within hours, an invitation to a cocktail party in honor of a Canadian financier who was in Washington for a series of talks concerning mutual problems of the Great Lakes.

Mrs. Garrison's secretary extended the invitation and at Barry's urging, rattled off a list of names of others who were expected. Among them was the niece of the Shah of Kushka, Elorith Modan.

On learning this, Barry accepted quickly. He had never met Elorith but had wanted to. He knew her to be an intelligent young supporter of her uncle's government and policies. It might be an excellent chance for him to discuss the situation in her country.

The first lead Lobo picked up was slim. It was the type of thing that he might have been tempted to ignore under other circumstances. But he knew the potential danger in this situation and he couldn't afford to overlook anything.

The International Peace Movement was staging a sit-in, maybe live-in would describe it more accurately, at Rock Creek Park. Hundreds of young people unrolled sleeping bags, set up camp stoves, and generally settled for an extended stay. Washington police, uncertain of how to cope with the huge crowd, had backed off with a wait-and-see attitude while the leaders of the Movement talked with city officials about their reasons for coming and their right to stay. The Peace Movement represented the voice of young America, it claimed, a voice that demanded to be heard. The march on Washington had been organized to bring that voice to the highest officials of government, including Congress, the Cabinet, and the President himself. The group planned to stay in the park until it had accomplished its purpose and gained its demands: that the United States remove all troops from Cambodia and Laos; all American armed forces be withdrawn from Europe and the

Panama Canal Zone; suspend operations of the nuclear submarine bases in Japan and England; withdraw from the Middle East; and finally, release the political prisoners to the National Liberation Army of Kushka.

As Lobo made his way over the jammed area that had once been well-kept lawn, he couldn't help wondering how any group could make such sweeping demands and expect them to be met. Did the IPM have any kind of force to back its words? Like maybe five canisters of deadly M-34 GB?

Lobo had taken the precaution of changing from his conservative slacks and sports coat to jeans and dark sweat shirt when he decided to investigate the park scene. He raked his fingers through his strawlike hair and let it flop carelessly about his face. He wished he hadn't shaved that morning but there was nothing he could do about that now. Hands in pockets, he slouched toward three men who seemed to be heading somewhere purposefully. He fell in step behind them with pretended indifference.

He caught snatches of conversation.

"—the fuzz off our backs."

"Man, like Fourth of July!" a tall, almost emaciated-looking youth in a fringed suede jacket said. The boy's face was covered with a bushy beard and moustache that flowed into his shoulder-length hair.

A dark, solemn-faced man darted a glance over his shoulder nervously. "For crissake, keep it down." He glanced about again then said something Lobo did not catch, except for the word "trouble."

The three cut away from the lolling groups on the grass and headed for Ross Drive. A white van was moving slowly close to the curb. Seeing it, the three broke into a trot. Two policemen patrolling stopped to watch the threesome, then moved toward them when the van stopped. Lobo paused, unsure of his next move. It could all be damned innocent—or at least as innocent as any

61

of this campy setup was, but the three had triggered his suspicion and he wanted to know more about them and what they were up to. He turned and fumbled in his pocket for a cigarette, lighting it while he watched the scene at the curb.

"Move along. This is a restricted area," one of the cops said. "You can't stop here." He slapped his palm against the side of the panel truck lightly. The driver, a sullen and scraggly blond with long hair and a beard, looked bored.

"Like, man, I'm just passing through."

"Move it."

The three had reached the van; the one in the suede jacket turned to the cops with something that might have been called a smile. "We're just unloading some food, man. The word's out that our delegation to the White House got permission."

The two policemen looked questioningly at each other. The youth pushed his advantage. "Now I know we don't have no permit or whatever but it's on its way, man. You ain't gonna make us send this stuff back? Judd here went to a lot of trouble to pick up the boxes and get 'em down here so's these brothers can eat today." He made a sweeping gesture with his hand toward the crowded park behind them.

The cop was clearly undecided, unwilling to take the responsibility of letting the group do something that might cause repercussions, yet even more unwilling to start trouble if it could be avoided. "Whatta ya think, Harry?" The other patrolman shrugged.

The nervous dark one hunched his shoulders and thrust his hands deep into his pockets. "Hell, you gonna make Judd do a second trip just because of some fuckin' piece of paper? Crissake, let us get the stuff out and he'll be outta here in five minutes."

"Okay," the cop said, "but I'll have to have a look at what you got."

The bearded one shrugged and opened the side doors of the van. A dozen or so cardboard cartons were piled inside, tops open and showing boxes of cereal, dry milk, flour, and similar staples. The three youths quickly began to pile the boxes on the grass. The two cops checked the first few, then shrugged and stepped back to let them unload the rest. The whole operation took less than ten minutes and by the time the last carton was out and the doors shut, the two policemen had already walked away, glancing back over their shoulders as they resumed their patrol. The panel truck rolled ahead slowly and waited for a break in the traffic, then edged into the stream.

The trio watched until it reached the corner then turned to the task of the cargo piled in front of them. The boy in the suede jacket put his fingers to his mouth and whistled sharply, waving an arm to the youths some hundred feet distant.

"Let's get a crew here to move this stuff!" he shouted.

The other nodded and in moments half a dozen jeaned youths came on the run.

"Cart this stuff back to headquarters," Suede Jacket ordered. He was in charge, organizing the newcomers to move the supplies.

Lobo blew smoke and squinted. It looked as if his hunch had been wrong. The van load of foodstuffs could hardly be considered sinister. He was about to turn away when Suede Jacket shagged two boys from some boxes that were slightly apart from the rest.

"Not those—we'll handle them."

The two helpers picked up the last of the other cartons and started across the grass. Suede Jacket waited until they were gone, shooting an inquisitive look in Lobo's direction at the same time. Lobo walked toward a group sitting under a tree around a guitar player.

From the corner of his eye he watched the three at the curb.

The last boxes seemed sturdier than the others and they were sealed shut. When the men lifted them, Lobo decided the boxes were very definitely heavier too. Two were alike in size, about two feet square; the third was longer by several inches, oblong.

"Jeez—be careful!" The nervous one grabbed for the box on his shoulder as Suede Jacket bumped into him accidentally.

Lobo waited until they were well into the crowd before he followed. His suspicions were up again . . . there was something about this. . . .

The three carried the cartons to the central campsite where a small tent had been set up and the other boxes of groceries had been stacked. Already, several girls were unpacking food and digging out pots and pans from a large cloth sack. The trio carried the heavy boxes inside the tent and Suede Jacket reached back to close the flap after them.

Lobo leaned against a tree and lit another cigarette. He couldn't shake the feeling that the boxes inside the tent were the real reason for the delivery and that the foodstuff had been camouflage. Why else would the three have carried them themselves, and why hide them instead of putting them out with the others? If he could only get a look inside the tent.

He watched a slim red-haired girl bend over a camp stove and try to coax it to life. He waited until she had made several futile attempts, then crossed to her.

"Need help?"

She swiveled her head, squinting as the sun hit her eyes. "Huh? Yeh, sure. This damned thing won't light."

"Let me try."

She looked about twenty, a slim curvy girl with gray eyes that would have looked better in a candlelit restaurant than in this wind-swept park. She shivered slightly, wrapping her bare arms across her breasts. She was wearing cut-off jeans and knit top, hardly enough to keep warm in the fresh spring breeze.

Lobo leaned over the Coleman stove, pumped air to the tank, then adjusted the valve. The burner caught as soon as he held a match to it. He sat back and grinned at the girl.

"You make it look so damned easy!" She made a face.

"If you call me a chauvinist, I'll turn the damned thing off," Lobo said, still grinning and reaching toward the control valve.

The girl grabbed for his hand. "Hey—no, I was only kidding!" She smiled then, and pushed at her hair, running her hand over it to smooth it. It was a useless motion since the wind whipped it back across her face almost at once. "What's your name?" she asked abruptly.

"Jeff. What's yours?"

"Sally." She looked as if she wanted to smile again but didn't. "You new? I don't remember seeing you around."

He shrugged. "I've been here. In and out. I've got friends in D.C. and I crashed there last night. I don't dig sleeping in the great outdoors when it's below 85°." He sat back and offered the girl a cigarette. She took it and he cupped his hands around a match and she bent to the flame.

"Yeh, it's a hell of a lot colder than I thought it would be. I'll be lucky if I don't get pneumonia."

He indicated the skimpy garments she wore. "That all you got?"

She nodded. "I came up from Georgia. Damn, I thought it was spring!"

Lobo set his cigarette on the grass and pulled the sweat shirt over his head. "Here, take it. You're getting blue around the edges."

She stared at him. "You—" She let it go and wormed

65

her arms into the sleeves. She yanked the sweater over her high breasts and shivered deliciously in its warmth. "Thanks. You're good people."

Lobo settled back and watched her mix something in a pot and set it on the stove. "Any word on the permits and stuff yet?" He glanced toward the tent.

Sally shook her head. "Freda's not back with the delegation yet. But there's no way the fuzz are going to move us out of here short of wholesale slaughter. And they're not ready to take a chance on that."

"What do you mean?" Did she know something?

She pushed at her hair again and stirred the concoction she had set to cook. It looked like a watery stew, but at least it would be hot. She looked at him sidelong. "Where'd you say you were from?"

"I didn't. But Philly, if it makes a difference."

She pursed her lips. "You know Burt Parker down there?"

Lobo knew he was being tested. He ran the file of International Peace Movement information through his memory in a rapid search. The Philadelphia sector of the group was headed by a man named Simon Mark, a youth director of an inner city recreational center.

He frowned. "Never heard of him. You sure he's in Sime's bunch?" He pretended to consider the name again.

"Yeh, well, maybe he hasn't been around lately." She concentrated on the stew again.

So he'd called her bluff and was safe for the moment. He settled to the grass, stretching his legs out. He jerked his finger toward the tent. "What's up?"

Her eyes went wide for a moment. "How would I know? Jeez, you sure ask a lot of questions."

He let it cool. It would do him no good to rouse suspicions. But it wouldn't do any good to sit around and wait for press releases either. He glanced at the tent. He could hear the low murmur of voices from inside, but the words were lost in the general hubbub of chatter surrounding them. What would happen if he simply walked into the tent? He could pretend it was a mistake, say he was looking for someone? Would the gambit work?

It was worth a try.

He waited until Sally moved toward several other women and busied herself with mixing a huge vat of powdered milk.

He got to his feet and walked casually toward the tent. Glancing around, he saw a small flurry of activity near the road but otherwise the marchers had settled down to their chilly wait for food. Lobo pulled at the flap, managing to untie the cord in a single motion, then jerked back the canvas. In the same instant, he ducked and barged inside.

"What the—" Suede Jacket whirled, ready to lash out. "Who the hell are you?" He stood, pushing against Lobo before he could get inside all the way.

"Seen Pike Longfellow?" Lobo said.

Suede Jacket looked surprised and angry. "No, I don't even know the goddamn jerk!" He shoved at Lobo's chest. "Now get outta here. This ain't no crash pad."

"Hey, cool it, man. Anyone can make a mistake. No need to get up tight." Lobo sidestepped and glanced at the boxes on the floor as he turned. They had been opened but the contents were still hidden under wrappings of cotton padding. Suede Jacket shoved him.

"On your way."

Lobo moved from the tent, mumbling as though irritated by the other's attitude. Outside, the flurry of activity near the road had erupted and a swarm of campers shouted and jeered as it moved toward the tent. In the lead were several armed policemen, guns and clubs raised to ward off attack.

Lobo was shoved to one side as Suede Jacket took a

better look at the advancing law. The man swore as he turned and ducked back into the tent. The police, a good score or more of them, moved quickly ahead.

"Hold it right where you are and there won't be any trouble!" a sergeant in front called. The cops spread out and surrounded the tent and cooking area. Guns were brought down and an uneasy silence fell. A few jeers came from the edge of the crowd but those close to the armed men were silent and watching.

The sergeant stepped toward Lobo, motioned with a shotgun for him to move away from the tent flap. The man pulled the canvas back and poked the nose of the gun inside. "Out with your hands on your heads!"

The three men in the tent emerged in single file. "Over there," the sergeant jerked the gun toward Lobo. "You, get those hands up!" Lobo complied.

Two cops entered the tent and came out a moment later dragging the three boxes. The cotton batting had been pulled back to expose stacked gas grenades and launchers. Lobo felt a quick tension in his guts. He'd been right about the trio. Gas grenades. Was there a connection with the stolen nerve gas or were these what they appeared to be on first glance? Tear gas? And how the devil had the police found out and moved in so quickly? Lobo remembered the two patrolmen who'd watched the unloading of the van. Had they called in to double check?

A blue-jeaned kid in a black jacket broke loose from the crowd and jumped one of the cops. It was almost like a signal, and the waiting mob surged into action. In seconds, fists and clubs were flying. Girls swung pots, clawed with bare hands. Men kicked and punched wildly. All hell broke loose.

Lobo pushed back trying to ease out of the thick mass of shouting angry young people. He could hear police whistles and new sirens in the distance. The raid had been well planned then, not a spur of the moment decision. The police had been tipped off and the bust was going to be big.

Hunched, he tried to slip through a small opening but was cut off when a new surge of thrashing kids filled the gap and pressed toward the police who were almost surrounded now. So far there had been no shots, but police sticks were raining blows indiscriminately. And the kids were fighting back with anything they could lay their hands on. Christ, if anyone got to those gas grenades—

Lobo tried to work his way back to the center of the mob but it was impossible. It was easier to go backwards now, the tide against him not as thick. Several girls had managed to form a circle around the overturned cookstove; the spilled stew had doused the flame of the burner and left a soggy mess on the ground. Lobo recognized a sweat shirt and saw the slim redheaded Sally on her hands and knees, face streaked with mud. He shoved his way to her and grabbed her arm.

She looked up, frightened at first then relieved as she recognized him.

"This way—" He pushed her along, wedging himself between rioters to force a path. She stumbled, almost fell several times, but he kept her on her feet. She looked thoroughly frightened now, her eyes wide and her face pale.

A bullhorn blared. "Break it up. Hold your fire, men!" The noise of the mob almost drowned out the voice. A second warning blared with little results.

Lobo was clear of the crowd, at the far edge where stragglers had backed off doubtfully. He could see the man with the bullhorn on a knoll beyond the heads of the throng. Uniformed, a cop. Then a girl pushed toward the man and said something; the man nodded and handed her the horn.

Her first words were swallowed up in the noise but after a moment Lobo realized she was gaining the attention of the mob. The pushing and shoving began to still and faces turned toward the woman with the bullhorn.

She was blonde with a round, animated face that commanded attention.

"—cool it! We've got our permit now, and we're going to stay until we get our rightful voice in the affairs of this country. Let's not screw it up now with a pig confrontation!"

A shout went up, some mumbling and restlessness. The blonde continued.

"Go back to your campsites now. We need to organize for our march tomorrow. Leave this trouble to me. I can handle it!"

Another stir of resentment swelled but subsided quickly. The crowd began to break up. Before his view of her was cut off, Lobo saw the blonde hand the bullhorn back to the cop with a triumphant look then move away.

Lobo turned back to Sally. The fear had left her face and she was almost smiling. "Who was that?" he asked.

She looked at him, surprised. "You mean you don't know Freda?" She shook her head. "Man, like you haven't been around the movement very long, huh?"

"Freda?"

Sally nodded. "Freda Polk. The International Peace Movement is her baby." She started to walk away, then turned to smile at him. "Hey, like thanks for the assist."

Lobo said nothing as he watched her walk back toward the ruined kitchen area. Freda Polk had vanished in the swirling mass of people. The police, once more in command of the situation, were carting off the three boxes they'd removed from the tent and the three youths who'd been in charge of them.

Chapter Seven

The television news was already carrying the story of the near-riot in Rock Creek Park when Lobo returned to the suite at the Carillon. He gave Barry his report, including a description of the gas grenades and launchers he'd seen in the boxes.

Barry whistled softly. "Do you think there's a connection?"

"I don't know, Barry. They were up to something, that's certain. I imagine it would be possible to transfer nerve gas from the original cylinders to smaller grenades—if you had the right people to handle it."

"And with launchers, a handful of people could lob grenades into every major government building in town. It could wipe out the city in minutes."

"Has there been any official word on the nerve gas?"

Barry shook his head. "The government is still sitting on the story. They've covered the incident at Gilmer with the accidental leakage story and it seems to be holding okay. There haven't been any other reports similar, so Gilmer looks like an isolated case. There's the usual speculation on how the gas got to that particular spot, but no one has zeroed in on stolen tanks. Dammit, Lobo, this thing gets stranger every hour. If someone's got the gas, it's about time for him to make it known. I can't believe those cylinders were stolen to be tucked away someplace and never heard of again."

"I have the feeling we may hear about them soon enough. When I got a look at those gas grenades today in that park, I thought maybe more than news was going to break."

They dressed for the cocktail party and took a cab from the side door of the Carillon. The driver stopped for a light and turned to watch fifty or more young people stream across the street. Most of them were carrying placards: International Peace Movement.

"Ever' year a new crop of nuts," the hack driver said, shaking his head. "There's hunnerds of those kids camping over at Rock Creek Park. I dunno why the cops don't run 'em off."

"You can't be against peace," Lobo said.

The driver turned his head, "How you spell that, friend? You oughta see what goes on over there. Screamin' and yellin' all night long."

The man shoved his cap back on his thick black hair and looked in the rear view mirror at his passengers. "You hear what those crazy kids did this afternoon? Damn near had a riot over t'the Park. Tear gas, Christ they had enough gear to start a goddamn war."

"I heard something about it," Barry said carefully. "It did turn out to be tear gas then?"

The driver snorted and the cab jerked ahead as the light changed. "Naw. Just troublemakers, that's all. The damned grenades were empty—can you figure it? Empty? They set up the whole deal with empty grenade shells! They *say* they wuz usin' 'em for scare tactics." He snorted again. "A lotta people can get killed with that kind of dumb thinking. And they march around with the signs saying they want peace. Dumb kids."

Barry glanced at Lobo and wondered if they were thinking the same thing. Empty grenades. Had the angry youth of the International Peace Movement been planning to fill them with nerve gas?

The entry hall of the Garrison house was crowded. The Canadian guest of honor had not yet made an appearance. Barry gave his name to an unsmiling butler, and he and Lobo were escorted to the door of the reception room. An orchestra was playing and there were

72

several bars busily dispensing drinks. The room was jammed with groups and with people wandering. The chatter and gossip were continuous.

Barry was recognized immediately and drawn into conversation with a number of officials and attachés and businessmen all eager for his words on specific programs or policies. It took him a half hour to extricate himself.

Lobo, in the meantime, had located Elorith Modan.

She was a beautiful woman in her early twenties; she looked at Barry over the rim of a tall glass. "So you're the famous Barrington Hewes-Bradford . . . ?"

"An accident of birth," Barry said, smiling.

"What a lucky accident." Her eyes ran over him lightly. "You're much younger than I thought."

"Young but very wise," Barry said, taking her arm and guiding her toward a corner. Elorith had a mysterious quality that he was curious to plumb. She was willowy, with an oval face and the huge dark eyes of many Eastern women. Her English was perfect. She wore several rings but none he could identify as a wedding band.

He said, "I'm very curious to hear your feelings on the unrest in Kushka. Is it serious?"

"In what way?"

"There is some talk of a coup."

She smiled. "It is an unrest caused by *your* country." She faced him, eyes dark as midnight and as impenetrable. Her tone was even, not bantering, but cool. Her flawless skin was vaguely olive and her black hair was severely drawn back. She was tall and wore a flowing sari-like robe that effectively concealed the curves he knew were there. Elorith would be a striking woman in any costume.

She smiled and slid the empty glass onto a table. "My country is very small, as you well know. If there were no oil under the sand, we would be nothing. We must be

73

very careful how we deal and with whom."

"Of course. The relations between your country and mine have always been excellent. Traditionally so. But suddenly they are strained."

"You are capsulizing, Mr. Hewes-Bradford."

"Barry, please."

She smiled faintly. "Barry. You Westerners tend to reduce everything to its essence. Rather than strained, let us say the balance has tilted for the time being."

"It has never been that delicate before."

"Times change," Elorith said. "If you will forgive a cliché. Your government has imprisoned a group of my people."

"Ah," Barry said. "We come down to it. They are not criminals but political prisoners. Is that the line?"

She made a face. "Perhaps."

"But you have no sympathy for those who break the law?"

Elorith looked slightly annoyed. "You are mocking me."

"Tell me your position."

"The prisoners you hold should be returned to Kushka."

Barry smiled. "Are we talking of the same thing? A small group of your countrymen placed a bomb aboard an airliner in an attempt to kill a handful of American officials who had nothing to do with oil disputes. Isn't that the case?"

She stared at him coldly. "The airliner was not blown up."

"But through no fault of the criminals."

Elorith smiled. "We're arguing like children. You are right. Neither I nor my uncle has any sympathy for criminals. But the Shah does support the high ideals of the National Liberation Army. He does not condone violence, but you should know that many among our people support the NLA."

74

"I see you do."

She shrugged lightly. "I have not said it. Do not jump to conclusions."

Barry decided to let it go. Elorith was apparently on both sides at the same time. He could not determine where her true sympathies lay. Perhaps she herself did not know. He glanced around. Others were moving closer, some doubtless curious about the private conversation. He took Elorith's arm again and they strolled, talking easily of nothing. They slipped outside to one of the several balconies, discussing Europe and especially Rome, where she had spent several months before coming to Washington.

The balcony was narrow and long and the curtains that were drawn over the French doors on the inside were sheer. Through them, Barry saw Lobo deep in conversation with a young blonde girl. She was properly dressed for the occasion, but Barry had the feeling she was not one of the Washington social types.

He turned back, giving Elorith a cigarette. Their eyes met as he lighted it and he found himself stirred by her look. He wanted to see her again—and he felt she knew it, maybe even shared the desire. Their talk never came close to personalities. Each time he brought it in that direction Elorith deftly evaded him like an expert fencer.

When they went inside again, Barry was surprised to see a group gathered around the blonde girl and Lobo. The girl was talking loudly, spouting an antiwar, anti-Establishment theme. Barry was instantly reminded of the placard carriers he had seen on the sidewalk earlier.

Lobo saw him and edged away. Joining Barry, he said, "That's Freda Polk, the persuasive voice of the International Peace Movement."

Barry hid his surprise. "She's on a soapbox tonight."

"I gather she always is," Lobo said. "Someone pushed the 'on' button." He smiled at Elorith.

Barry introduced them and Elorith glanced at the blonde girl in the midst of the crowd. "I must go."

"Let me see you out." Barry took her arm and they moved toward the door. "Are you remaining in Washington?"

"I—I do not know."

"I would like to see you again. Where are you staying?"

"At the Embassy, for now."

Two men whom she introduced as attachés were waiting for her, and Barry could do little but bow stiffly and watch her disappear.

Freda Polk had concluded her impromptu speech and Barry was surprised to see that Lobo had smoothly detached her from those eager to ask questions and was bringing her across the floor.

Lobo introduced them. "Freda has been wanting to meet you, Barry."

"*You're* the famous Barry Hewes-Bradford?" She was obviously astonished. "I thought you'd be an old duffer with white whiskers! Or are you Bradford Junior?"

"I'm the only one," Barry assured her. "I heard part of your remarks—"

"And you didn't agree with any of them."

Barry smiled. "I thought you presented them well." Freda was not a beauty, perhaps not even pretty. She had a round, peasant face and a sturdy, capable-looking body. She looked slightly out of place in the long gown, as if it were unfamiliar garb.

She smiled. "Well, you make a more attractive enemy, I must say. We should get together and exchange viewpoints sometime. I'd like to hear more about the rich point of view."

"Are you sure?" Barry asked. "Would it influence you?"

She laughed. "I doubt it. But it'd be fun. Why don't you ask me for a date?"

Lobo grinned over her shoulder and Barry smiled. Freda Polk was quite a different sort of girl from Elorith.

"A date to talk politics?"

"Doesn't that interest you?"

Barry shrugged, not caring to commit himself. Freda was interesting, something of a challenge. He knew the arguments and had listened to her kind before. He had little time to debate the merits of the democratic system with her. But she *was* the leader of the International Peace Movement. And talking about that might lead to information he needed.

"I'm sure we could find more interesting things to discuss. May I call you?"

She laughed. "They haven't put the phones in at Rock Creek Park yet."

Barry narrowed his eyes and let his gaze move quickly over the gown she was wearing. A momentary flush caught her round cheeks and he knew she realized the absurdity of her lie. She had not readied herself for this party in the kind of tent in the park Lobo had described.

"On second thought, maybe we wouldn't have anything to talk about, Mr. Bradford." She turned away and ignored the arm Lobo extended to her. Moments later she had been cornered by a young politician Barry recognized by sight.

Lobo turned to Barry. "I wonder how she managed to get invited here tonight?"

"Freda Polk is a complicated young woman, Lobo. I think we'd better try to find out more about her."

Chapter Eight

In the middle of the afternoon a news bulletin interrupted the on-going television program on every channel.

"Bulletin:

"This station has just received a communication purported to be from the National Liberation Army of Kushka and signed by its leader Ali Yashar. It states that the NLA has in its possession five canisters of nerve gas, stolen from U.S. Government depots in various parts of the country. The NLA two weeks ago demanded that the five men being held in connection with the attempted bombing of an airliner last month be released to the Kushkan government. The demands have not been met and the communication received claims that the NLA will use the stolen nerve gas to enforce its demands.

"No official statement has been made as yet on the communication or that any gas canisters have in fact been stolen. High sources, however, indicate that recent activities at several gas-storage depots may indicate such thefts. Our White House correspondent is standing by to bring any further bulletins as soon as they are issued."

The bulletin brought a storm of protest and an avalanche of calls demanding more information. Regular programming was suspended on the three major networks as reporters quickly arranged on-camera interviews with senators, congressmen, generals, and presidential aides. The so-called communication from the National Liberation Army was hogwash and completely untrue, said several informed sources.

While on the air, a spokesman changed his story, attempted to recover, and was twisted in his own words by an experienced interviewer. Yes, there had been unrest in Kushka but it was being handled. He had nothing to say about the gas canisters.

All news-reporting media had received the NLA communication but it had not been sent to the White House. Attempts were made to ascertain the truth of the statements that nerve gas had been stolen. A Chemical Warfare officer, whose name was withheld, asked a reporter to delete the word "stolen," and substitute "missing."

Later the same hour the officer retracted the story and insisted there were no canisters missing, stolen, or misplaced.

The television networks dug into their files for the Gilmer story. A poison scare had alerted the citizens of a farming community near Gilmer; five men had died there under mysterious circumstances. It was known that the Government had sealed off the area but the resultant findings had not been released. The Pentagon reported this case was still classified. It denied that nerve gas had been the cause of the deaths.

One of the networks dug an old documentary out of the archives, dusted it off, and presented it: The Effects Of Nerve Gas. It ran fifteen minutes and alarmed the viewers as nothing else had.

Barry received Tom Radley's report that same afternoon. Radley had received no cooperation at all, had indeed been threatened with jail if he continued to pry into "government business." Radley had interviewed everyone who knew of the Gilmer affair and had paid a deputy sheriff, a man named Uchitel, a hundred dollars for a secret discussion that he guaranteed would not be used in the press. It was Uchitel's opinion, based on what the county medical examiner had said in his presence, that the five deaths in the lonely field were caused by nerve gas.

Tom Radley and the others were recalled. Barry had no doubts concerning the nerve gas. Frank Trask reassigned the men, asking them to discover all they could about the National Liberation Army and Ali Yashar.

A second bulletin, delivered to all TV stations and newspapers two hours after the first, stated that if the demands of the NLA were not met within seventy-two hours, a canister of nerve gas would be released in an American city.

Panic exploded.

A high government spokesman was forced to admit the loss of the five canisters. "But everything possible is being done to recover them."

Media commentators speculated that if the first canister did not do the trick—in bringing about the release of the prisoners in question—then the remaining canisters might be released, resulting in widespread deaths—perhaps millions.

This did not help.

The President went on the air, begging the press to censor itself, to use judgment in reporting, assuring the populace that everything was being done to contact and deal with the NLA. The NLA, he said, was using the airwaves to blackmail the government. No American city was in danger.

Commentators continued to discuss the problem on

the air, vying with each other for tidbits of news. The attempted bombing of the airliner containing five American officials, as well as a hundred other citizens, was reviewed and film shown. Pictures of the five prisoners held by the U.S. government were also given wide publicity. The tiny sheikdom of Kushka was dissected on the air and the oil dispute which had ostensibly started the entire matter explored in depth.

The Hewes-Bradford interests were discussed along with others, and reporters contacted Hewesridge, asking for interviews with Mr. Barrington Hewes-Bradford. They were told Mr. Hewes-Bradford was unavailable.

Very few of the reporters discussed the National Liberation Army itself—because none of them knew anything about it and its aims. Its leader, Yashar, was also unknown. There was a rumor that he had attended a university in the United States but no one knew which one. Yashar was quickly becoming a household word.

The third communiqué from the NLA, signed by Ali Yashar, was the most damaging, from the standpoint of national peace. It contained the serial numbers of the canisters, as proof that the NLA actually had the gas. It reiterated the ultimatum that the five prisoners be released, and added the demands that all Western oil interests get out of Kushka immediately and that the American Sixth Fleet in the Mediterranean be recalled.

Barry, along with five other executives of leading oil companies dealing with Kushka, was ushered into the President's Oval Office.

The aide said, "The President will be with you in a moment."

Barry stood beside Alex Hammond, president of Conrio Oil. Hammond was looking well. They had met last at the International Alpine Tennis matches at Kitzbühel, Austria, the previous August. Barry asked about Mrs. Hammond, but before Alex could answer the doors opened and the President strode in.

He shook hands with each of them. "Thank you for coming, thank you for coming."

Barry said, "How are you, Mr. President?"

"Hello, Barry. Glad to see you again." The President indicated chairs. "Please be seated, gentlemen." He went behind the desk. "Please smoke if you care to." He smiled. "What's a little more smoke in the air?"

They laughed politely.

The President clasped his hands together and leaned forward across the desk. "I'm very interested in your opinions, gentlemen. You all know the situation, probably as well as I do myself. What can you tell me about Kushka?" He looked directly at Barry.

Barry said, "In our opinion, my own and my company's, Mr. President, we have confidence in the Shah."

"You do not anticipate a take-over?"

"By force? No, sir. The Shah is an experienced campaigner. I grant you he is along in years, but his son, Prince Eqbal, is a serious, responsible man."

Alex Hammond said, "We believe it is possible the Shah has isolated himself from reality. We're somewhat concerned that the National Liberation Army may have made more inroads than the Shah's government suspects."

The President nodded. "We have conflicting reports from Kushka. We tend toward your opinions, Barry, that the Shah is capable. But that leads us to the conclusion that Yashar is bluffing about the oil companies and the Sixth Fleet."

Barry said, "He may be, sir. But can we take the chance of calling the bluff."

"Exactly. It's a high level poker game."

Dennis Gillimore, executive vice-president of Greening Oil, said, "Mr. President, is there any doubt that Yashar has the cylinders of nerve gas?"

The President frowned. "This is not for official publication, gentlemen, you realize that. No, we have no doubts. We've been investigating the thefts of the tanks for five days. It's incredible, but we have no leads whatsoever." He shook his head. "This entire scheme seems to have been worked out far in advance and was well organized. That's why we are so anxious to find out if the government of Kushka is behind it or if Yashar is working on his own." He looked at each of them in turn. "It could make a great deal of difference in the final outcome." He got up slowly. The five men in the room rose. "I would be very much obliged, gentlemen, if you would keep me informed of the local situation as you see it in Kushka. Your communications many times are better than ours." He smiled and went down the line, shaking hands again. "Thank you very much, thank you—" He went out.

National and local politicians were swamped with calls. In a number of instances masses of people crammed families and possessions into cars and trucks and headed out of the cities. New York had the worst traffic jams in history, as did most of the eastern seaboard cities.

A small March On Washington started in a Virginia county. No one seemed to know how it began; people came into the streets spontaneously and began the march and by the time the front-marchers gained the outskirts of Washington, the mass of people had grown to fantastic proportions. Alarmed, the authorities called for soldiers. An entire brigade was flung around the Capitol itself, seemingly the target for the march.

Pitched battles were fought. Hundreds were hurt and a dozen or more taken to jail.

One of the marchers, provided a microphone by a network television newsman, hysterically demanded that the President of the United States deal immediately with Yashar to avoid the threatened mass killings by deadly gas. The cry was taken up by thousands.

The White House was stormed by rioters; the crowds were thrown back with difficulty by police and additional soldiers rushed to the area. Washington, D.C., was placed under martial law.

By nightfall the city lay under an uneasy truce. A number of fires were started and the night was made even more restless by the continual sirens. The President went on the air, pleading with the nation to resist the thoughtless agitators. A meeting *was* being sought with the blackmailers; a solution would be found.

Then a rumor sprang up and spread like wildfire that the first city to be the target of the NLA was Philadelphia.

On the telephone with Trask, Barry asked, "What's the situation, Frank?"

"I was about to call you. We have news. Tom Radley has been spending money under the counter. He's come up with some interesting bits. The wreck of a truck was found in a gorge not far from a place called Gandy. Tom's positive it's the truck used to steal the canister from Point Archer."

Barry asked, "How does that help us?"

"The wreck had a hydraulic lift and inside were the remains of a motorcycle."

Barry was interested. "A motorcycle?!"

"Yes. Tom says a switch was made there, near the gorge. The stolen canister was put into another vehicle and the truck was dumped. The men, or some of them, went over the hills on motorcycles."

"One man was killed—so they had to dump one bike."

"Affirmative." Frank's voice held satisfaction. "Now, the three men killed near Gilmer—Red Miller, Jake Stacton, and William Scoey—were the men who rode the cycles. It all fits together."

Barry said, "Not yet it doesn't."

"Because I left out one piece. The three were traced to a town called Cutler and into the garage of a man named Pringle. The motorcycles are there and the fingerprints check."

"That's damn good work," Barry said, "no matter how Tom did it. Where's Pringle now?"

"He's disappeared. We think Pringle is close to Yashar. There's evidence he knows him at least." Frank chuckled. "But there's more. The other three were in the can with Pringle five years ago. That's a definite tie-in."

"What about the fourth man, the one killed at Point Archer?"

"Nothing on him. I suspect that's why they left him behind. Nothing tied him to the others. According to the prison records, Pringle was a cut above the others in brains. That's about it, Barry."

"Very good. Tom deserves a bonus. But keep him digging, Frank." Barry was already wondering if he could use some of this new data to pry more information from Fritz.

"What's the situation in Washington?"

"Bad. Everyone's shaken up. We've got a form of martial law that restricts movement, but I doubt it'll last. People are getting out of town. I think some of the panic is over. The government is doing more than people realize, but it's hard to convince them."

"D'you have to stay there?"

"I'm hoping for information through several sources."

"All right. We'll keep trying to track down Pringle. Of course the government boys are, too. Tom says he's stepping on FBI men on his way to the bathroom."

"My guess is Yashar will hole up. He must be a thousand miles away." Barry sighed. "If you can find what college he attended there might be a photo of him."

"Affirmative. We thought of that. But with all the publicity you'd think the college itself would come forth. It hasn't."

Barry grunted. "That means he attended under another name. Keep it up, Frank."

He called Fritz de Bausset. Fritz was out; his secretary was happy to take a message. Barry left his code-name: Orchard.

He had barely hung up when the security man called. Lobo took the call, listened, and turned to Barry with a surprised look. "Freda Polk is downstairs. Do you want to see her?"

Barry was even more surprised. "Freda Polk?" He hesitated, then said, "Send her up."

She came in almost demurely, looking around as if the suite were strange and unearthly. Barry wondered if it was a pose. Freda was capable of anything. She wore a dark patterned jacket and a long skirt with sandals. Her blonde hair hung straight to her shoulders. She smiled at Lobo but went straight to Barry. "Hello, remember me?"

"Of course, the rabble-rouser."

She laughed. "Don't underestimate us, Enemy of the People. We'll get you yet."

"I should drop you out of the window right now and save us all a lot of trouble later. Would you like a drink?" Barry saw Lobo smile and leave the room silently.

"Scotch and water, thanks," Freda said and sat down looking at the fireplace. "Thanks for seeing me, incidentally. I s'pose you know what I want."

He made the drink and took it across to her. "No, I can guess, but you tell me."

She shrugged. "I want you to use your influence to get the prisoners released to the NLA."

First Elorith, now Freda. Why had she selected this cause from her crusade's long list of demands? He sat down opposite and smiled. "What influence? The government doesn't—"

"Bullshit," she said with an almost explosive sound. "You're one of the most powerful men in America. You can make things happen."

"You overestimate me."

"No. I know your track record." She sipped the drink, then smiled. "But I don't want to fight—not about that, of all things. Would it be so awful to save millions of lives?"

Barry tried not to let his annoyance show. Of course she was baiting him. He wondered if she and Elorith were together on this thing. It didn't sound possible but one never knew; Freda did seem to have connections. He said, "Tell me what you really think."

She looked at him and made a sound that was almost a snicker. "I really think you're one of the most dangerous men in America."

"Dangerous?"

"To us. You're enormously attractive, you know."

"How does that follow?"

She laughed. "One speech from you at a gathering and half our women would desert us." She rose and came over to him. "Do you think I'm exaggerating?"

"Of course." He smiled, feeling himself slightly off balance and thinking that was what she intended. "Tell me about this Peace movement of yours."

"It started as a religious crusade. My father is a preacher, you know. We were living in Denver when he started all of it. Now it's called the International Peace March . . . or Movement, take your pick."

"Is he still connected with it?"

"Father? Hell no. He got disgusted with the lot of us and pulled out." She laughed but her eyes were steady.

"A lot of younger blood got into it and it's changed. We *have* to do something, you know. There isn't much time."

"You don't get along with your father any more?"

She shrugged. "He's a man of the last century, not this one. He wants to save the world by bringing it back to God and the simple life. He doesn't realize that times have changed. We're realists."

Barry said, "Are you sure?"

"Will you help free the prisoners?"

Barry took her empty glass, got up, and crossed to the bar. "The prisoners are criminals, of course. You recognize that?"

"Who the hell cares?" Her voice held anger again. She could go from caress to anger in one wink of an eye. "Our lives are at stake! Isn't it stupid to be talking about right and wrong instead of survival?"

He looked at her round face set in an expression of defiance. How much of it was a pose? He made the drink and took it to her. "I haven't anything to do with the negotiations. And if you know politicians, you'll know that's the truth. There's too much white heat on them now. If I, or anyone else, approached them it would do no good. They don't want anything to look like coercion or special interest suggestion." He smiled. "They'll have to handle this one themselves."

She gazed at him pensively, her expression saying she was unconvinced. "Are you really against war?"

"Of course I am!"

"I don't believe you. How could any man with your interests, especially in oil, really be against war?"

Barry sighed. Who was it who had said, "You can't win them all"? He said, "Are you really for peace?"

She blinked. "What the hell d'you think?"

"I think you believe what you want to believe, despite the facts."

She said nothing, sipping the drink. Then she

laughed. "Can I call you Barry?"

"Please do."

"It's getting late." She finished the drink and slid the glass onto the coffee table. "D'you mind if I stay the night?"

"What for?" Barry asked, with a straight face.

She looked at him, eyebrows level. "On second thought, I don't know either." She got up and started toward the door. "I don't suppose you'll help us either . . ."

"Getting the prisoners released?"

"What else?"

"No, there's no way I can," Barry said. "I'm a disappointment to you all the way around."

Freda nodded. "To me you're a pain in the ass."

Chapter Nine

The pursuit of Yashar was making little headway. The news bulletins were unfailingly bad and Frank Trask's men had turned up nothing new.

"Yashar's been reported in a dozen places, Barry," Frank told him on the phone. "The rumor about Philadelphia has everyone jittery. I think the entire country is on the edge of hysteria. The police report that armed robbery and assaults are up alarmingly."

"There's no tomorrow," Barry said, almost in an undertone. "I wish we had a picture of Yashar."

"I've got five different descriptions of him," Frank said. "It's fantastic that he was able to avoid cameras all his life."

"Get Martin Becker on it, or have you already?" Becker was the Hewes-Bradford manager in Kushka.

"Affirmative. We contacted him, Barry, and he'll see what he can come up with. But I still think our best bet is the U.S. school, if we can locate it."

"Don't stint."

"There is one thing—only a rumor. Do you want to hear it?"

"Hell yes!"

"It concerns Denver, Colorado."

Barry grunted. Denver was close to the Rocky Mountain Depot, a storage place for hundreds of canisters of nerve gas. The depot was one that had not been raided. He tapped his fingers on the leather-topped desk impatiently.

"Denver is one of the places where Yashar has been reported. But also—" Frank paused as if to accentuate the dramatic importance of what he was about to say. "Several people have reported seeing gas canisters, or at least one, in various parts of town."

"What?!" Barry was unprepared for this.

"That's right. And the descriptions tally. People have described the real canisters pretty accurately."

"Send Tom Radley down."

Frank chuckled. "I already have."

Barry tapped the desk, staring at the opposite wall. It was only a rumor. But several people had seen *something*. He made up his mind. "I'm going to Denver myself, Frank. Have Tom contact me at the Winterford."

Frank sighed. "Wilco, Barry." He rang off.

In the Star Jet, Barry listened to the news broadcasts with Lobo. The nation had been near hysteria but there were definite signs that the panic was subsiding. People could put up with the idea of imminent destruction just so long. Then it became familiar. They had been threatened with something so horrible that the mind had trouble coping with it—but nothing had happened. The days slipped by; they were still alive, and now despite the NLA deadline, normality was slowly returning.

The police in every state had been augmented by the National Guard and by reserves. Crime diminished quickly and people began returning to normal pursuits. There was a feeling, beginning to be voiced by commentators, that the elusive Ali Yashar and his invisible Army of Liberation were unstable. They did not want to negotiate with the government, proved by the fact that they did not come into the open and that they chose to present their demands to the press and not to the authorities. The White House had never received a communication from Yashar that had not first been sent to the press. And no arrangements had been outlined for a meeting with the militants.

Barry listened, wondering if this made Ali Yashar less dangerous. The man *did* have the nerve gas canisters. He had verified this by releasing the serial numbers. Yet his main thrust seemed to be urging the mass of people to force acceptance of his terms.

So far Yashar had said nothing about what he would do if the government acceded to his demands. Would he turn over the canisters? Could anyone trust such a man?

In the mile-high city Kel Grodin brought the Star Jet in smoothly as a robin and set it down on the runway at noon. Lobo got them a cab and Tom Radley was waiting in the lobby of the Winterford Hotel. Barry signed the register as B.H. Canfield and took a suite on the fifth floor.

Tom Radley was a man of medium height, wiry and tanned. He seemed somewhat younger than his forty-six years. He looked like a schoolteacher. He was the kind of person who blended inconspicuously into any group. He was a method actor, he told them, imitating a chameleon. His gray eyes were deceptively bland behind tortoise shell rimmed glasses.

To Barry's question he said, "We haven't been able to substantiate the rumors that Yashar is here because no one I can find knows what Yashar looks like. It's not easy to track down a name without a face and known habits."

"What about representatives of the NLA?" Lobo asked.

"No one admits to membership," Tom said dryly. "If he did, the gent would probably be lynched. We checked out Pringle's friends and came up with nothing. Pringle was a loner. Your friend Yashar has covered his tracks well."

"But the tracks *are* there," Barry said pensively.

"What about the government agents?" Lobo asked. "Are they making any progress?"

Tom shrugged. "I know most of them—the old hands anyway—enough to pry out some information. Ali Yashar heads the militants but I don't think they number very many. Frank Trask and I figured that there might be a hundred or more here in this country. Now I suspect twenty . . . maybe less."

"That means they hired outside men to do the actual raiding." Lobo frowned. "Four of them were found dead. What happened to the others?"

Tom said, "I suspect they're dead too. For a very good reason. The four you mentioned were all men with records. The rest probably have, too. Now I ask you, can a man like Yashar afford to have them around, able to finger him and the NLA? If someone walked into the office of the FBI with a photo or a good description of Ali Yashar and his operation, he could probably name his own figure for the information, correct?"

Barry nodded. "If you're right, Tom, that's progress of a sort."

Tom Radley adjusted his glasses. "I think our best bet here in Denver is the canister thing."

"Go on," Barry said.

"I know about four reports that cylinders of gas have been spotted." Tom smiled. "I grant you, people will be seeing canisters in their alphabet soup. Everyone's jumpy. The mayor's been on the air trying to calm them and warning people not to take the law into their own hands."

"Where and how were the canisters seen?"

"All on trucks. Of course the trucks are gone by the time the police arrive and no one has a license number." He consulted a note. "The trucks have been a small moving van, a flatbed, a two-ton, and another van."

"Not much," Lobo said with a sigh.

"There's one positive thing about these reports," Tom said. "The first two came in to the police before the news broadcasts described the canisters. I got that from a friend who knows."

Barry cocked his head. "And the descriptions were accurate?"

Tom nodded.

Lobo said, "If they *are* the right tanks, or even if one is the right article, why is someone allowing it to be seen on the streets?"

"A damn good question," Tom said, looking at Barry.

Lobo growled, "Maybe we're dealing with nuts."

"Yes, they're nuts," Barry agreed, "but on a high level. I notice you said, 'allowed.' Is it possible someone *wanted* the canister to be seen?"

"To create panic?" Lobo said. "Like the kind of idiot who starts forest fires or the nut who commits the duplicate of a crime he's seen on a TV show?"

Barry nodded thoughtfully. They certainly could not discount the idea.

Tom said, "I ought to call in, talk to my police contact." He glanced around the room for a telephone. Lobo pointed to the next room and Tom went in. In a moment they could hear his monotone.

Lobo took their bags to the bedrooms and returned. "I should check with Frank, too."

Tom hurried back. "There's been another call! A woman swears it's the real thing—"

"Let's go." Lobo went to the door. "Tell us on the way, Tom. D'you have someone on it?"

"Yes, Jerry Howe, a local private cop."

They went out to the elevator. When it came it was noisy with a clatter of teenagers and they said nothing at all in the car. Tom beckoned, "I've got a rented Ford around the corner."

They followed him. "The cops have sealed off the block and are combing every corner." The woman who had called in had been awakened, she said, by a noise in the alley behind her house. She looked out the window and saw some guy closing the doors of his panel truck. It took her a couple of minutes to realize what she'd seen and by that time the truck was pulling out.

Tom unlocked the trunk of the rented car. "I've got a couple of old jackets here." He glanced at Lobo and Barry. "Better shed the fancy duds."

"What did the truck look like?" Barry peeled off his jacket and laid it in the trunk. He extracted a pair of large sunglasses from the pocket and slipped them on.

"Dark panel job. She only had a glimpse of it. She can't remember the color."

Lobo asked, "Any lettering on the side?"

"She didn't see any." Tom slammed the trunk lid closed, nodding approvingly at the change in the others. The shabby coats made a great deal of difference in them. He slid under the wheel and turned the key.

It took fifteen minutes to drive across town. It was a shabby section, once a community of light manufacturing and tract houses; the area was rapidly degenerating. A few small factories still operated; there were rusting auto bodies in front yards, peeling paint, and almost no greenery.

Tom parked the car and they got out. The street was blocked by a police car; there were a dozen cops visible, in the yards, the streets, making a thorough search. The watching crowd was becoming disinterested. The police seemed to be interested in one particular house at the end of the street where there was a house trailer in the driveway near the rear of the lot.

Tom Radley grunted and indicated a short man on the other side of the street. The man walked casually toward them. In an undertone, Tom said, "That's Jerry Howe, my man."

The short man, hands in pockets, approached. "Got a match, pal?"

Radley dug in his pocket and brought out a book. He cupped a flame to the cigarette Howe put between his lips. Through a small cloud of smoke, Howe said, "I think I got something for you."

Radley signaled Barry with his eyes. "Let's hear it," he said.

Howe turned so he was facing the street again, to all appearances nothing more than a curious bystander. His voice was low, clearly audible to the three men close to him but not carrying beyond them. "See the red-headed kid by the fence over there?"

Barry glanced toward the gray house where a sagging fence circled a miniscule yard. The boy was about six or seven, a thin-faced, big-eyed kid who looked as though he'd never learned to smile. From time to time the child glanced at the small knot of boys near the barricade almost wistfully. He was obviously not a part of the gang.

"He was playing down in the alley, he says. Doesn't want his mother to find out because he was told to stay in his own yard. Says he saw the canister."

Barry kept his glance casual but his interest perked instantly. Once again he mentally commended Frank Trask for putting Tom Radley on the detail here. Tom, and anyone who worked for him, would uncover things the police had missed.

"Says the guy who lived in the trailer down there had it in a truck."

Radley said, "Did he know the man?"

"He's seen him around the neighborhood. Name's Harry. The guy's only lived in the trailer a few weeks. Seems like a bum, never had a car or truck before. That's why the kid watched; he was surprised to see the guy doing something different. He was putting stuff inside the truck, like maybe he was going on a trip."

"Suitcases?" Radley asked.

"One, a beat-up valise, seemed to be heavy. The boy says the guy had trouble lifting it into the truck. That's why the door was open as long as it was. Steve, the kid, says he saw the canister plain as day then. It was lying sideways, in some kind of box." Jerry Howe glanced

©Lorillard 1973

Micronite filter.
Mild, smooth taste.
America's quality
cigarette.
Kent.

King Size or Deluxe 100's.

Try the crisp, clean taste
of Kent Menthol.

The only Menthol with the famous Micronite filter.

briefly at the three men close to him. "The boy swears there were pipes and hoses attached to the end. He says they looked like the kind of things he's seen at the hospital. Got hit by a car last year and was taken to emergency. He remembers all the gruesome details of the emergency room pretty clearly."

Barry kept a poker face. "Could it have been an oxygen tank? Maybe a welding outfit?"

Howe said, "Steve claims he knows the difference. Says the tank in the truck was bigger, more than twice the diameter. I couldn't shake him on that." He inhaled deeply, then blew smoke. "It fits with the call the woman made. She described the tank just about the same, except she didn't notice the pipes or hoses."

"What about the truck itself?" Tom asked.

"Steve says it was dark green. I got a license partial from him. The last three figures are 228." Howe pulled a bit of paper from his pocket. "The kid wrote it down himself." He passed the paper to Tom.

Barry said, "How about the police? Do they know this?"

Howe shook his head, "No, sir. Steve didn't tell them because he's nervous with cops. And because he's afraid his old lady will give him hell. He was supposed to be in his own yard at the time." He glanced at Barry and Lobo. "It's not my job to uncover info for the police as long as Mr. Radley's paying me."

He had asked no questions about the men with Tom, Barry noted. If Howe had any idea of their identity he did not let on. Apparently if Tom Radley had brought them, they were okay. It was testimony to Tom's reputation.

Radley put the scrap of paper in his pocket. "Okay, Jer. Stick around in case anything else falls on you."

"You bet," Howe said and ambled away.

Chapter Ten

Radley's men were efficient. Jerry Howe and another were tracing the movements of the man who lived in the trailer, crisscrossing police trails and branching off on their own as fast as they could. They reported they had a picture of the suspect, obtained from the police artist who had done it according to descriptions given by neighbors.

Other operatives set out in search of the panel truck. Armed with the child's description and license partial, they were one step ahead of the police. During the drive to Radley's apartment, Barry speculated that the truck would need special springs and fittings in order to carry the heavy load of the cylinder. Radley agreed and said his men had been told to pay close attention to garages, body and fender shops, and the like. If the truck had been fitted commercially, they'd find out where the work was done.

One of Radley's men called about an hour later. The truck had been seen on Jamison Street and the man had located a large vacant warehouse that showed evidence of recent use. Inside, he'd found a spraygun containing maroon paint and spattered newspapers that had been taped over windows. There was a good chance the truck they were looking for was now maroon. In a trash can the operative had unearthed a crumpled stencil smeared with yellow paint. GLOBE TV.

"Sounds like a break, Barry," Radley said as he hung up the phone and relayed the information. "At least now we think we know what we're looking for."

Radley paced the apartment, smoking one cigarette after another. "If the cops ever find out I didn't give 'em that partial license, they'll want my blood . . ."

It troubled Barry also—but it might have led to very embarrassing situations. That was one of his major problems, keeping himself personally out of such investigations. If his cover was once blown, he was finished for good as a viable force. He could send the police anonymous information but in the past he had found that they tended to discount it or did not act quickly enough. If a man on Barry's payroll was involved in secret machinations, it might reflect on him. Therefore Lobo or Frank Trask handled most investigations—through other persons. Tom Radley, for instance, paid his snoopers by roundabout methods. And Tom was on an H-B payroll as an insurance adjuster.

Jerry Howe located the maroon truck forty minutes later and phoned in. "It's parked on a downtown street," he said. "The guy's in it, just sitting there."

"Waiting for something?"

"I dunno. Just sitting."

"Just a sec," Tom said and looked at Barry, who had heard both sides of the conversation.

Barry said, "Tell him to stay put. Don't let the truck out of his sight."

Tom nodded, got the precise location, and told Howe to stay on watch. He hung up. "What do you suppose the guy is up to?"

"How busy are the streets at this hour?" Barry asked.

"Crowded, as a rule," Tom Radley said. "You figure he *wants* to cause a panic?"

Barry shrugged. "He may be sitting there getting his nerve up." He headed toward the door. "Let's go."

Lobo sprang up. "Wait, Barry—we've taken it far enough. Let's let the police grab the guy—it's their business—I mean we can't handle this by ourselves. We're not equipped to. What if that nut opens a valve?!"

Barry looked at Tom who nodded agreement. Barry said, "I think that's exactly why we have to do it ourselves. What happens if he sees uniformed police converge on the truck? The man will panic. We may be able to find a way to get to him before he knows anyone has spotted him."

Tom said, "He may have a radio in the truck, tuned to police broadcasts."

Lobo grumbled all the way down to Radley's rented compact. There was no sense, he said, in Barry's risking his life in this kind of operation. He and Tom could handle it or bring in other men.

Barry knew that Lobo was quite capable, but he could not withdraw and let others do the job just because there was risk; and he knew Lobo understood that, despite his grumbling. Barry considered the possibility the man in the maroon truck was in the middle of the city to release deadly gas, killing himself as well as thousands of others.

Did the elusive Yashar believe the nation needed a lesson in bargaining? Would Yashar deliberately massacre innocent masses to force a decision? Illogical acts had been committed in the past and would be again, no doubt. Was Yashar so lacking in humanity that he could order one of his zealots to mass murder?

Barry could not make up his mind. It did not make sense that the NLA would carry out a threat before the deadline had passed. And yet—what *did* make sense to a man like Yashar?

All three of them might be riding to their deaths. Barry felt the prickles rise on the back of his neck. Lobo's face looked set and stern under the cropped yellow hair. Tom Radley, at the wheel of the car, was hunched and tense. Barry knew both men were aware of the odds and the consequences.

The maroon truck was parked on Welton Street, in the very heart of the city. Barry asked Tom to drive past it so they could take a look. There was a shadowy figure in the cab, sitting perfectly still. It was not a new truck; despite the recent paint job it still looked shabby. The sides were dented, a fender twisted. It was similar to hundreds of other panel trucks. Was the tank of M-34 GB in the back? There was no way to see inside.

Tom circled the block in moderate traffic. There were no parking spots. Barry said, "Pull over a half block behind him and let us out. Give us time to get to the truck, then move by slowly. Cut him off so he can't pull out."

"Gotcha," Tom said. He leaned forward and opened the glove compartment. Barry saw two short-barreled revolvers. "Better take them." Lobo took them and slammed the compartment lid.

Barry frowned, then pocketed one of the pistols. He didn't like the idea of shooting but maybe Radley was right. There might be no choice. "Thanks."

On the sidewalk he said, "We'll have to play it by ear."

"I'm nervous," Lobo growled. "Let's go."

They walked slowly past the buildings on the street. Barry studied the van as they approached. Was the driver watching them in the rear view mirrors mounted on either side of the cab? Barry felt a trickle of sweat between his shoulder blades. It was risky but they had no real choice. The important thing was to get the guy out of the truck before he could do anything about the cylinder in back.

"If we pass him and come back, he's going to get suspicious," Lobo said.

"We won't pass him. Soon as we get close to the truck, we'll cut behind it. You make a grab for the rear door, see if you can get inside to the tank. I'll try for the driver."

"He may start shooting."

"That's a chance I'll have to take. Let's hope Radley can distract him for a couple of seconds."

They were only yards from the van. Barry felt the familiar surge of excitement that danger brought. When they were a few feet from the truck, Barry angled into the street, still moving casually in case the man in the van was watching. From the corner of his vision he saw the rented Ford approach. He paused, stepping back as though to let it pass. Behind him, Lobo was already at the rear doors of the van, twisting the handles. Barry didn't wait to find out if he got them open. He cut close to the truck, pretending to watch the traffic coming up behind him. He slipped one hand from his pocket and put it to the door handle. He readied the gun in the other.

The Ford cut sharply in front of the panel truck. Barry saw the driver's attention drawn to it. He quickly depressed the latch button and pulled the car door open. The man inside whirled, eyes wild.

He was an older man than Barry expected, probably in his middle fifties. He had sunken cheeks and badly needed a shave. He yelled, "Get away!"

Barry showed him the pistol. "Climb out of there—nice and easy." He tried to sound tough.

The man shook his head. His thin face was pale and drawn, eyes bloodshot and red-rimmed. He looked as if he had not slept for days. His longish hair was streaked with gray and flopped carelessly about his head. He was dressed in rough clothes, shirt open at the neck.

"Move back!" the man screamed again. "Go away or it will be too late for all of them!" He raised his hand and showed Barry a clenched fist. From it ran a thin cable. The man's thumb was pressed against a red plunger; his knuckles were white.

Barry stared. He realized instantly the man had prepared himself for just this contingency. No matter who approached, or how, the man could manipulate the plunger before he was overpowered.

The man yelled, "When I let go, the gas will be released!"

Was he bluffing? Barry felt the cold caress of fear at the back of his neck. Was the cable rigged to set off the gas in the canister? He could see nothing in the back of the truck. Lobo had not gotten the rear door open.

"Take it easy," Barry said. "Why don't you climb out and we'll talk about it?"

The other shook his head and the long hair flopped in a tangle. "It's too late. The world is corrupt!" His voice was a wail, rising like an old time preacher's. "Evil has poisoned the minds of the nation!"

"Won't *you* be evil if you kill with that gas?"

"It's too late." Dark brows pulled together in a scowl. "God is not mocked! The world must pay for its sinful ways. The world must pay . . ."

Barry felt Lobo's presence behind him. The man in the cab moved restlessly as he became aware of the newcomer.

"Stay where you are—" He showed the plunger again.

Barry put up a placating hand. "All right, take it easy." He moved back. "No one's going to hurt you."

Lobo hissed, "It's locked—can't get in the back."

"The nation must come to its knees before God! Evil and corruption must cease! Peace—God's way is peace!"

Barry frowned. The man seemed beyond reason now. He was breathing hard and sweating as his fervor grew.

People had stopped on the street, office workers and tourists, shoppers and the curious—chattering and staring. "What is it, Mac?" a man asked. Lobo shook his head.

Ahead of the maroon truck, Tom Radley got out of the Ford and put up his arms. "All right now, let's move along—please move along—"

Most moved, shrugging and grumbling. A few men stood their ground. "You a cop, mister?"

Lobo came to help. "Let's keep the sidewalk clear." The men looked at him and decided not to make an issue of it.

Barry kept his eyes on the zealot in the truck. Was it coincidence he had picked this time to carry out his wild scheme? Or was he fronting somehow for the mysterious National Liberation Army—a decoy to distract attention from something else? *What* something else?

The hell of it was they couldn't take a chance it was only bluff. Tom and Lobo had moved the curious along but the danger was just as real. If this nut *did* have a tank of nerve gas, releasing it could wipe out the city.

He thought of rushing the guy and pulling him out of the cab before he knew what hit him, but the zealot had the seat belt securely fastened about his middle.

"Go away—!" he shouted, waving his arm. "It is the Day of Judgment! The day of the Lord has come!"

He raised his hand toward the windshield threateningly. As though suddenly realizing the danger, the crowd pressed back and a murmur of alarm swirled upward. A few people at the edges of the knot bolted, running across the street, dodging past the Ford that blocked the truck. A woman shrieked and fell as she tried to push past the tight group behind her. In seconds, the crowd was near hysteria.

Lobo sidled toward the back of the truck but the man in the cab saw him. "Stop! Stay where you are! The moment is here. Make peace with your God before it is too late! Too long the world has not listened!" The hand rose again.

Barry dived into the cab, sprawling over the driver's lap as the man released the plunger. Barry lunged for the wire, feeling fingers claw at his neck and face.

The next moments erupted with a violence that triggered full panic in the crowd. The rear doors of the panel truck sprang open, released by a hidden catch. A loud pop—then a hissing sound.

"Too late! Vengeance is mine saith the Lord!" The fanatic fell forward over the steering wheel, limp suddenly. Barry jerked away, raced to the rear of the truck. The gaping doors showed a large cylinder supported in a wooden and leather-strapped crate that was bolted to the floor. The stenciling on the head of the tank stood out boldly: M-34.

"Move them back! Fast!" Barry shouted but Lobo and Tom Radley were already dispersing the throng as quickly as the crowded street would allow. Traffic had come to a standstill, drivers gaping from windows, then trying to race through the jammed street as they realized what was happening. Screams pierced the din.

Barry grabbed one of the open doors and tried to slam it shut over the hissing gas. He couldn't force it against the thick cable. He was within feet of the tank now and his eyes began to sting and tear. He coughed and sputtered for air as the acrid fumes assailed his eyes and nose. He held his breath, aware suddenly that smoke was pouring from the underside of the truck, billowing up and creating a screen.

The crowd was pushing and shoving as panic drove them in search of safety. Still coughing and sputtering, Barry realized the hissing gas was tear gas! Not the deadly nerve gas he had expected! He had been in the cloud for several seconds and there was no indication of the muscle spasms the M-34 GB would have produced.

They had been duped.

Sirens wailed, approaching fast. Barry stumbled through the dense smoke back toward the cab of the truck. Groping, he found the door and reached inside. The driver's seat was empty. He felt quickly along the floor, opening his eyes to slits to make sure the man had not fallen. He was gone, escaped in the pandemonium he had created.

Barry moved toward the Ford. Lobo ran to him, grabbing his arm. "Are you all right, Barry?"

"Yes—" The word tore from his raw throat. "Get Radley—" Lobo sprinted away.

105

Barry leaned against the car, trying to force the coughing spasms to quiet. The gas was mixed with the billowing smoke, rising above the engulfed truck like a signal to the world.

Radley came on a dead run with Lobo. "Let's get out of here," Barry yelled.

The two men grabbed Barry's arms and, heads ducked, began running away from the truck. Barry had to depend on the others to guide him. He could not see from his irritated eyes. It was all he could do to breathe.

"Through here." Radley pulled them into an arcade. The long corridor was empty now, an open elevator standing ready. Everyone had rushed to the street to see what the excitement was, then been carried away with the hysteria. Radley seemed to know where they were and he led them through the building. They emerged on a side street. He paused and let Barry lean against the wall a moment. "You okay, boss?"

Barry nodded, breathing deeply as the fresh air soothed the inflamed tissues of his nose and throat.

"Tear gas," Lobo said. "God, what kind of a nut would dream up a stunt like that!"

"I'd better call this in. That crowd is in a state to panic the whole damned city!" Tom headed for a phone booth in the lobby behind them on a dead run. Minutes later he was back.

"I called a guy I know at police headquarters. They'll get the word out to the TV and radio stations and alert all units. Let's hope no one is killed before the truth sinks in."

Barry patted his eyes with the handkerchief Lobo produced. His chest felt like hot coals but he could breathe all right. A fire engine roared along the street in front of them, sirens blaring. When it passed, Barry said, "Let's get out of here. I want to learn more about this fanatic and just what he was up to."

Chapter Eleven

Pandemonium prevailed in the streets. In the downtown district, cars were halted, causing massive traffic jams. People left the stalled cars and ran. Word of the gas had spread like wildfire. No one wanted to die.

But no one seemed to notice that people were not collapsing in droves, dead on the spot.

In fifteen minutes the cool night air had worked its medicine. Barry's eyes no longer burned and he could see normally. They were out of the district where hysteria had taken over. Police were everywhere, setting up lines, directing traffic, and closing off the area where the maroon truck sat. A sound truck passed them, blaring its message: "There is no need for panic. Repeat, there is no cause for alarm. Please remain calm. No poison gas has been released—no poison gas has been released. Turn on your radio or television for news bulletins. Do not panic. There is no cause for alarm . . ."

The truck passed, endlessly reciting its message. There were no cabs to be had but Tom Radley led them back the way they had come. The police were busy clearing the streets of abandoned cars—it would be an all-night job, Barry could see. Tom walked past several, then returned a few moments later driving a small Chevy.

"Found one with the keys still in it."

"In addition to your other crimes," Lobo said.

Tom looked toward the nearest policeman. "Come on, get in. We'll bring it back." He put the car in gear as they jumped in and slammed the doors. "Back to the hotel, Barry?"

"No, I want another look at the trailer where our friend lived."

"The cops'll be there," Lobo objected.

"I doubt it. Not after the general alarm that's out."

Tom asked, "You think he'd risk going there?"

"I don't know," Barry said, "but it's the only lead we've got. He's on foot and he's wanted. He may have money hidden there. He'll have to go somewhere."

Tom worked his way toward the edge of town. They could hear the sirens as ambulances and police cars wailed, heading for the downtown district. Probably a number of people had collapsed from shock and would have to be hospitalized. Barry switched on the car radio and quickly found a station broadcasting bulletins.

". . . incident near Civic Center in downtown Denver is under control. Police urge citizens to remain calm. There is no danger from poison gas. We repeat. There is *no* danger from poison gas. Experts have determined that the gas released was only tear gas. Police have no explanation at this time why the tear gas was released. It may have been a malicious prank—or something worse. At latest count fifteen people were injured in the panic that took place. Two are dead of heart attacks. Scores of automobiles have been abandoned and all downtown streets are impassable. Do *not* go into the downtown area. We repeat, do *not* go into the downtown area, please. The tear gas is still strong. If you are in the downtown area at this time, please remain indoors. Keep doors and windows closed. The tear gas will disperse soon but if you are suffering discomfort, do not rub your eyes. Rinse with cold water or an eyewash. We repeat, there is *no* danger.

"Police believe one man was responsible but they are also on the lookout for several others who were noticed near the truck from which the tear gas was released."

Barry turned the broadcast off. "What about your rented car?"

Tom sighed. "I'll have to phone someone to go and claim it. The cops'll impound it for now."

"And we'll find the impound fee on your expense account," Lobo remarked. Tom laughed at the weak joke. Reaction was setting in.

The street that had hummed with activity a few hours before was silent and deserted. The shabbiness of the neighborhood seemed even more pronounced. The police barriers had been removed.

Tom Radley parked the borrowed Chevy near the corner and the three men walked toward the driveway. There was no guard at the trailer. Apparently the police had written off the incident as a false alarm.

Barry circled the silent vehicle and came back. His voice was low. "I want a look inside."

Lobo said, "The police will have cleaned it out, Barry."

"Keep watch for a sec," Tom said. He moved to the door of the trailer and began to work on it. Barry heard small clicks and metallic sounds; Lobo walked toward the house. It seemed deserted.

Tom said, "Hiiiiist—it's open." He passed Barry a small pocket flash.

Opening the door, Barry eased himself inside the slightly creaking vehicle. It smelled stuffy; there were food odors and some he could not identify. He clicked on the flashlight when the door was closed behind him. Shades had been tightly pulled on all the windows. No light from the outside entered. There was a table, two padded benches, the usual built-in stove and sink—and one other thing.

A body. The man was on the floor, lying on his side, as if he had tried to ease pain by curling into a fetal position. Barry knew instantly he was dead. He recognized the thin face with the long, graying hair matted about it. Bloodshot eyes stared at nothing. It was the man who had driven the maroon truck.

He went to the door, clicking off the flash, and beckoned Tom Radley. "We've found him."

Tom came in, bent over the figure, and touched the man's skin with fingertips. "He hasn't been dead over half an hour."

Barry said, "It's our friend with the tear gas."

Tom moved, examining the body quickly without moving it. "Knife through the heart. Looks like someone came up behind him."

Barry knelt and stared at the hilt of the blade. It protruded only a few inches from the dead man's back, an ordinary brown handled knife, the kind of kitchen utensil that could be purchased in any hardware store. Whoever had killed him had done it expertly and left no trace of his identity. Chances were the knife had come from the tiny kitchen of the trailer. Had the killer been waiting here in the dark?

Radley straightened and moved the light over the interior of the trailer. It was one room, with a folding bed along one side, the table wedged at its end. The minute kitchen was no more than a sink and stove, with a refrigerator built under the counter. Dirty dishes were piled in the sink and there was a faint aroma of stale coffee clinging to the air. At the other end of the room, the drawers of a built-in chest were ajar, as though searched quickly.

Barry motioned toward it and Radley moved closer with the light. He removed a handkerchief from his pocket, pulled the drawer open, and went through it quickly. He repeated the process on each of the other drawers, then turned and shook his head.

Barry pointed toward the drapery that hung on a wire. Pulled back, it revealed a makeshift closet that contained several dark shirts, a worn jacket of nondescript color in the dim light, a pair of dark slacks. Radley went through the pockets of each garment methodically. Nothing.

Barry had the feeling that if there had been anything here, the killer had taken it to erase any tie to himself or the dead man's activities.

Radley came back to the figure on the floor. He knelt, careful to avoid the small pool of blood that had collected close to the body. He patted the dead man's pocket, reached into the coat to double check. He shook his head. "Cleaned out. Not even a wallet or keys." He got to his feet.

"Okay, let's get out of here. The police may start thinking the same way we did as soon as the excitement dies down."

Barry waited until Radley clicked off the light, then opened the door. From a house nearby, angry voices shouted in a domestic fight. It was an effective cover for the soft sounds of their retreat.

Back in Tom Radley's rented apartment, Barry and Lobo sat at the small formica table in the kitchen. Radley busied himself at the stove, preparing steaks for the broiler.

"I hope you like steak and salad, that's about all I've got."

"Fine," Barry said. Radley had insisted on fixing a meal. They had been on the go since noon and, if anything else broke, it might be hours before they had another chance. They needed energy.

Radley was at ease in the kitchen and he enjoyed exercising his skills. Cooking was something of a hobby with him and when he was at home in Chicago, he often prepared gourmet dinners for friends. Here in the furnished apartment there was little space or equipment for more than quick meals but he had taken the precaution of laying in a supply of tenderloins and salad-makings.

111

He had to spend time here waiting for reports. Now he was pleased to have a chance to fix a meal for Barry and Lobo.

At forty-six, small pleasures such as this were important to Radley. His job with Hewes-Bradford Enterprises was his life. He had no family to demand attention and he devoted almost all his energy to doing his work well. He was proud of his record as one of Trask's operatives and he accepted the fact that he was at the top of the list. He worked hard to stay there.

He pushed the broiler pan under the flame and turned to the sink where the washed greens were heaped in a colander. He began tearing lettuce and dropping it into salad bowls.

The phone rang. Radley turned, wiping his hands on the towel he'd tied around his middle.

"Yeh?"

"This is Simons, Tom. Got something on the guy in the trailer."

"Let's have it." He was already reaching for a pencil and the pad of paper he kept near the phone. He took notes while Simons relayed the information he'd uncovered. Several times Tom asked questions. Five minutes later he hung up the phone and went back to the kitchen. Lobo grinned at him from the sink where he was finishing the salads.

"That was Simons. We've got something, don't know how much good it is."

"Anything is better than the stalemate we're at now," Barry said.

Radley glanced at the steaks under the broiler before going on. "Vehicle registration shows the truck belonged to Jeremiah Polk of Temple Street."

Barry sat up. "Did you say Polk?"

Radley nodded. "Yeh, that mean something?" The name had not struck any familiar notes in *his* memory but Barry seemed to recognize it.

Barry glanced at Lobo as he carried the three salad bowls to the table. "Didn't Freda say her family came from Denver?"

Lobo nodded. "Got anything more on him?" he asked Radley.

Radley translated his shorthand to words. "He's a minister, no church connection now. His last church was the Assembly of Heaven over on Delmondo Road. He got himself tied up with some group." He checked the scrawls again. "International Peace March. It began in his church and he was the driving force. Seems he got carried away and the church finally cut its ties with him, let him go."

Barry nodded. "That matches the story Freda told me. What's he been up to lately?"

"No one knows. He lived alone at the Temple Street address. Neighbors there say he was a loner, stayed to himself. Sometimes they didn't see him for days on end. Matter of fact, no one of his old group has laid eyes on him for a few weeks. Some thought he'd moved out but the landlady says his rent was paid up till the end of the month." Radley turned and grabbed a potholder and drew out the broiler pan so he could turn the steaks. He began setting the table while he talked. "That seems to fit with the time he's been at the trailer."

Tom moved to the stove and removed the steaks. The aroma of the sizzling meat filled the tiny kitchen and he realized suddenly how hungry he was. He'd had nothing since breakfast and that had been a very long time ago.

He slid the steaks to plates he'd warmed in the oven and carried them to the table. The three men attacked the meal with gusto. They were silent for a time, then Radley picked up his report.

"I told Simons to trace Polk's history. He may be able to come up with something tomorrow. It's pretty late for much more tonight."

Barry nodded and chewed a piece of steak. "The

113

thing that worries me is the way that canister had been rigged to look exactly like the stolen nerve gas. I don't think it can be coincidence."

Lobo said, "You think there's a connection with Yashar?"

"Yashar could be in town," Radley said. "We can't rule out the possibility anymore than we can prove it."

Barry was thoughtful a moment. "It could be a red herring."

"What do you mean?"

"A show of power, letting us know what kind of panic can take over if people believe the nerve gas is going to be released. Polk is a known radical and a fanatic to boot. He could have been set up."

Tom thought he knew what Barry was getting at. "You mean the guy was used?"

"Yes. He talked only about the day of judgment—no reference to the NLA demands. I think someone planted the idea in the old man's head that he was taking a stand for peace. It was his chance to give people a warning of the kind of vengeance that they were bringing on themselves."

"But why use Polk?" Lobo said. "Is there a connection between that peace group of his and the National Liberation Army?"

"Freda Polk has a hell of a lot of sympathy for Yashar and him cause," Barry said.

"Should I know this Freda Polk?" Tom asked. He might be able to follow up on her if she had a connection with Jeremiah.

"She's been making a lot of noise around Washington the past few weeks. One of these young radicals that feel any means justifies the end if it's peace. Rallies, protest marches, you know the sort of thing."

Radley nodded. "And she came from Denver?"

"That's what she says. And her father started the International Peace Movement in his church. Some of the young people thought the old man wasn't moving fast enough, so they branched out on their own, with Freda out front waving the banner."

Tom whistled softly. "You say she's in sympathy with Ali Yashar?"

"She thinks the United States government should release the Kushkan prisoners as Yashar demands. Her logic is that it's in the good of peace and that's the thing that really matters."

"If it stops there." Tom finished his steak.

Barry nodded. "I have the feeling that Yashar didn't go to all the trouble of stealing five canisters of nerve gas to stop at that point. I'm afraid that meeting his demands would take away our only bargaining power and put us in more danger than we are now."

Tom frowned. "You think he has other plans for the gas?"

"We can't afford to risk the possibility. It could be the start of something a lot bigger. We've got to locate those tanks and dispose of the gas." He glanced at Tom, then at Lobo. "I think Lobo and I had better get back to Washington. You and your men can handle things here."

It wasn't a question but Radley offered an answer. "Sure. We should have something definite by early afternoon tomorrow. I'll keep in touch with Trask."

"Call me directly unless it's so hot it has to go through the scramble phone," Barry said. He pushed his chair back and smiled. "Now how about a cup of coffee to top off that delicious steak?"

Grinning, Tom Radley rose for the pot.

Chapter Twelve

Barry woke early despite the fact he'd had little sleep. He had relaxed on the plane and again when he and Lobo had returned to the Carillon in Washington. A call to "Whitehead" had elicited no information. There were only routine messages waiting for him; he had decided to wait for morning to check with Frank Trask again.

Lobo called down for breakfast to be sent up. Barry clicked the television set on. A news bulletin had apparently been made public earlier and a commentator was exploring it in more depth.

". . . another communication from the militant National Liberation Army terrorists who stole five canisters of deadly nerve gas. The communication was sent to all radio and television stations, received at six this morning. As before, the NLA message was not sent through official channels.

"We quote the exact message as received by this station this morning: 'The National Liberation Army of Kushka reminds the people of the United States that thirty-six hours of the seventy-two are already gone. If the prisoners are not released before the deadline we have given, the nerve gas will be used. There is no way the gas canisters can be discovered to prevent this. The United States Government must meet our demands. We will not bargain. We will listen to nothing but the joyful cries of our free comrades. Free the prisoners, get out of

Kushka, and remove the Sixth Fleet from the Mediterranean Sea. These three things we demand. Only your compliance can prevent tragedy. If tragedy comes, it is the fault of the United States Government. You will bring this upon your own heads.

" 'Because the capitalist government has delayed so long, we the people of the new liberated Kushka declare that our land is no longer open to Americans. Tourists and Americans living in Kushka will be given twenty-four hours to leave. Any who fails to leave will be taken into custody.' "

A bell chimed and Lobo went to the door. The announcer continued.

"That was the end of the communication from the NLA. As far as we can tell there has been no official comment on this latest NLA harangue. White House correspondents report that the President has been engaged in round-the-clock meetings. Attempts to contact Prince Eqbal of Kushka have failed and it is not known at this time whether or not Kushka has suffered a military takeover.

"It has been learned through reliable sources that the United States Government has not put in motion the mechanics of releasing the prisoners in question."

Barry turned the sound down as the station went into a commercial. A white-jacketed waiter had wheeled a cart into the outer room. Lobo slipped the man a tip, then brought the cart into the living room.

"Sounds like Yashar is getting edgy. His time is slipping away," Lobo said. He pulled up the sides of the cart and drew chairs to it. "Will the government give in?"

"It's pretty damned risky without a chance to bargain," Barry said. "What assurances do we have that Yashar will turn over the gas? So far he hasn't done anything to show good faith."

They ate in silence for several moments. Barry said,

"It's bad news if all Americans are run out of Kushka. Prince Eqbal and his father have always been fair-minded men. I find it hard to believe they'd be taken in so completely by Yashar."

"You think Yashar may be lying?"

Barry shrugged. "There's no way of telling unless we get some inside information."

"Martin Becker?"

Barry nodded, finishing his breakfast and taking his coffee across the room. Reaching for the phone, he dialed Hewesridge. Vera Crawford came on the line.

He said, "You've heard the latest bulletin?"

"Right, boss. It sounded a little more hysterical than the others. D'you want Frank?"

"Yes." There was a click and Frank Trask's crisp voice spoke in his ear. "Hello, Barry—I was about to call you."

"Morning, Frank."

Frank's tone was decisive and efficient. "I have a call in to Martin Becker in Kushka, Barry. There's a delay on the lines but the operator says she can complete the call. Apparently telephone communications haven't been cut off."

"How authentic do you think this latest ultimatum is?"

"I was wondering that myself. We have no information at all that Kushka is in the hands of the so-called Liberation Army. This may be a bluff. I've been trying to get through to the Shah himself or his advisors. So far no luck."

Barry said, "Hmmmm." He was wondering if Becker, the H-B manager in Kushka, would be able to talk freely if Frank got him on the line. Becker was a Swede. He might be able to stay in the country. But if the ultimatum *was* made good, then all the employees of foreign companies would probably be given walking papers.

118

He said, "I want to know what kind of arrangements are being made for the safety of our employees if the NLA does kick them out."

"Affirmative, Barry."

"We'll also need to know how much business we'll be able to conduct if worse comes to worst."

"I'm preparing a statement on equipment and ships."

"All right, Frank. I think it's imperative for us to find out if the Shah has been deposed. We must have contacts who can—"

"Give me a little more time, Barry. Right now the situation seems totally confused but it may not be."

Barry agreed. He filled Frank Trask in on the details of the incidents in Denver. "I told Tom Radley to call me or Lobo directly. He'll file reports with you later. I don't want to lose a second if we can get a jump on Yashar."

"I understand. We're still checking colleges. Have you any idea how many of them there are in this country?"

"Yes," Barry sighed. "It may be a waste of time but keep at it. Maybe we'll get lucky. Anything else?"

"Whitehead called last night. He thought you might want to know that one of the five Kushkan prisoners is a top demolition and chemical warfare expert."

Barry groaned. "That *is* news!"

"The guy was a scientist in a government sponsored project at Tophanger during the Korean War. You recall that's where the GB gas was perfected and production began."

"He's not an American?"

"No. Name's Josef Draggett. He was born abroad but educated in U.S. schools. Scholarship to Ohio State, graduate work at M.I.T. He went to Kushka in '68 on a visit—his mother's people were from there. He dropped out of sight in '71. Appeared next when he was captured a few months ago in the plane bombing attempt."

"Okay, Frank, keep in close touch."

Barry hung up and frowned. He sipped coffee, staring at the wall. He related the news to Lobo who shook his head.

"Letting this Draggett character out of jail may be the match they need to light their fire."

Barry nodded, "There's a damned good chance of it. He may be more dangerous than the gas. If the White House knows this it may be why there's been no official statement on the ransom demands. Stealing tanks of nerve gas is one thing but handling it safely is another. The incident in Gilmer may have scared Yashar enough to cause him to up his demands to get Draggett out."

"The key to something big . . ."

"Yes, maybe using the gas somewhere. I wonder what the chances would be of Yashar taking a canister of gas to Kashka?" He shook his head. "No telling with a man like Yashar, of course."

Barry picked up the phone and dialed Fritz de Bausset's private line. Fritz answered himself, "Yes?"

"Orchard here, Fritz."

"Hello, Mr. Orchard." Fritz was crisp and guarded. "You've talked with Frank?"

"Yes, thank you. One other thing. What about the situation in Kushka? Is it stable?"

"We've been in communication with the skipper of a Japanese tanker who just sailed from Kushka. He reported the city quiet. Troops are patrolling but the Shah is still in command. You heard the news broadcast?"

"Yes. It's a bluff?"

"We think so, Mr. Orchard."

"Thank you very much." Barry hung up and grinned at Lobo. "Yashar *is* getting desperate."

"That makes him dangerous as hell."

"Yes, it does." He paused. "I wonder if Freda Polk

120

could give us any leads. Think you could find her and bring her here?"

Lobo smiled. "I could try."

"Then get on it. The faster we find out if Jeremiah Polk had connections with the Kushkan Liberation group, the faster we may be able to find that gas."

Lobo headed for the door.

Lobo returned with the blonde girl about an hour later. Freda was wearing a pair of cut-off jeans and a sweat shirt. Her long hair hung straight, giving her a teenage look that was far removed from the seductive young woman who had come to his apartment a few nights ago. Her dark eyes were smouldering with something other than passion.

"You rich bastards are all alike," she said with almost a snarl. "Snap your fingers and the peasants are supposed to come running. Well, I haven't got much time, so make it fast."

Her attitude surprised Barry and he tried to win her over with a smile. "Thanks for coming. I was hoping I had convinced you the last time we met that I wasn't all bad, as you seem to think."

She laughed harshly. "No, not bad," she said with a cold smile. "But you're still Establishment, Barry. I don't suppose you'll ever be anything else."

"Is that so terrible?"

Her eyes narrowed and her face darkened with the rage that was seething in her. "You and your rotten Establishment killed my father!" She spat the words at him.

She knew about it then. How? An official notification from the authorities, or the wildfire communications of the movement? Barry pretended surprise. "I thought your father lived in Denver?" He put the right amount of concern in his voice.

121

She whirled and walked several steps from him, then turned to face him defiantly. "It's the same rotten Establishment. He never had a chance."

"What happened?"

She laughed, a mirthless sound. "The cops shot him down. Poor crazy old coot, he never had a chance."

Barry didn't have to pretend surprise this time. If Freda believed her father had been shot by police, her information had not been official. "Tell me about it."

She shrugged and tugged at the bottom of the sweat shirt. "Pop got some crazy idea that he had to save the world from going to hell. Seems he decided on a scare tactic, threatening that he was a forerunner of the doom that was to come. He had a harmless tank of tear gas—" Her face twisted and for a moment Barry thought she was going to cry. Her eyes clouded but no tears fell. "No one would listen to him. Some jerks rushed him and he panicked. They shot him down without giving him a chance!"

Lobo glanced at Barry who said, "I heard about an incident in Denver but the facts don't jibe."

She snorted. "Yeh, I heard that 'official' story too. A cover-up. It was the police who panicked. And they killed a poor old man who never harmed anyone in his life. Look, I know my father. Sure he's—was—a little odd but he was no killer. He devoted his whole life to trying to bring peace. I tell you he really believed it! He thought he was a messenger of God, his assignment was to spread the good word." She broke off and a sob caught in her throat as she turned away again. "Peace! Sure, but it has to start somewhere." She shoved her hands into the jeans' pockets and rocked on her heels.

"What did you want to talk to me about?" she asked without turning.

"Have you been in touch with the militants of the NLA?" She was in no mood to be coaxed, so his best chance was to strike directly.

She turned, frowning and her lip caught between her teeth. "What the hell business is it of yours?"

"Freda, you've got to listen. This isn't a kid's game. You can't put an end to this thing with a few banners and slogans. The deadline Yashar gave is damned near up and—"

She came at him with a fury. "Tell the President! Why hasn't there been any move to release the political prisoners?"

Barry shook his head. "They're dangerous criminals—"

She made a rude noise and stalked away again. Lobo would have yanked her back but Barry shook his head. She was already antagonized enough. It would do no good to try to force her to listen.

"All right, that's out of our hands. Neither you nor I can do anything about that, it's an official decision. But you can help by telling me anything you know about Yashar and his movements."

Her eyes narrowed. "Tell *you*? Is it just idle curiosity? What's in this for you, Barry?"

"For Godsake, don't you realize what a keg of dynamite you're sitting on? Are you willing to risk killing innocent people just because you don't like the way the government is running things?"

"The government is willing to risk innocent lives to save face. They can't admit they were wrong in not turning over those men to Kushka. If they had, none of this would have happened! Tell that to your friends in high places!"

Barry wanted to grab her and shake some sense into her but he knew that would only enrage her further. She had closed her mind and ears.

Freda smiled grimly. "Maybe some day you'll understand," she said. "There is a chance that peace will come in our time but only if governments stop playing God. Until then, I guess you and I are walking on different sides of the street." She turned toward the door. "I have a protest march on the White House organized. Sorry to cut out this way but I'm willing to go out and stomp for the things I believe in. This time we'll make ourselves heard!"

She walked out, not bothering to close the door behind her. Lobo followed, closed it, then turned back to Barry.

"Not much," he said. "She's a wildcat."

Barry rubbed knuckles across his chin. "Find out what the official story released from Denver is. I want to know where Freda got her information. I'm beginning to think she may be a lot closer to Yashar and his liberation army than she lets on." He looked at the door, "And put somebody on her. I want to know where she goes and who she sees."

Chapter Thirteen

News filtered in slowly during the day. Powerless to change the situation, Barry became restless. He paced the suite endlessly and littered the ashtrays with discarded butts.

Frank Trask reported he'd spoken on the phone with Martin Becker. "None of our people in Kushka have been harmed, Barry. There's been a lot of hollering and chasing around but no military take-over."

"Yashar's bunch are not strong enough?"

"Not at all. The Shah's soldiers are everywhere. Martin says they marched into the plant and offices to give us protection in case . . . and they're also protecting all the men's families. But nothing happened. Yashar just doesn't have the clout in Kushka. The streets are quiet."

"Can you get through to the Shah?"

"Negative. Martin says he can't reach any high officials. But that doesn't mean anything for the present."

Barry said, "Hmmm. It could mean the military's already in the driver's seat."

"I suppose so but Martin thinks not. He's on the spot and his judgment is always good."

The television showed footage of Freda Polk's protest march on the White House. She had massed several hundred young people armed with placards; the mob had surged down Pennsylvania Avenue chanting slogans and raising fists in a mixture of the peace and militant power signs. A company of special detail police had blocked their progress, forced them behind street barriers and tried to hold them there. Tempers flared and fighting erupted. When ordered to disperse and fall back, several dozen youngsters had thrown themselves on the ground and refused to budge. These had been carted off, kicking and shouting, to police vans. There was a close-up of Freda Polk, screaming imprecations at the police, but she was not one of those loaded into the vans.

Tom Radley called from Denver shortly after noon. His men had uncovered the origin of the tear-gas tank in the maroon truck. The tank itself, Tom said, had been built for bottled gas. A serial number stamped on the bottom had been traced to a small gas company that serviced a number of trailer parks on the outskirts of the city.

There had also been a recent robbery of a police training academy. Tom's theory was that the tear gas had been stolen from the academy well in advance, more proof of the careful planning of which the NLA zealots were capable. Tom had no idea how the tear gas had been transferred to the tank. Stenciling the Chem Warfare code on the tank was easily done.

Scraps of lumber matching that used in building the frame for the tank were found in Jeremiah Polk's trailer. There was little doubt, according to the local police, that the elder Polk had put the apparatus together and driven the maroon truck. His fingerprints were found all over it. But there was no trace of the persons or person responsible for the plan. Tom thought it was likely Jeremiah Polk had acted alone.

Barry asked in surprise, "You mean you think he *might* have acted independently of the NLA group?"

"I think someone proposed the idea to Polk and planned it out for him but he was left on his own for the act itself."

Barry sighed. "And killed to wipe out any chance of tracing his activities back to the source."

"That's what it looks like."

"Any news about Yashar?"

"Rumors, Barry. But so far I haven't been able to convert any of them to fact."

Barry paused, worrying his chin. "Why not concentrate on Polk's death? See if you can track down the killer before the police do. It might provide us a lead."

"Wilco," Tom Radley said and rang off.

How many hours were left of the time Yashar had allotted? He was about to discuss it with Lobo when the phone rang again.

Lobo picked up the receiver and spoke; he covered it, "Elorith Modan."

Barry smiled, "I want to talk to her." He reached for the receiver. "Elorith—"

"Hello, Barry." The voice on the line was soft and hesitant. "I've got something to talk about . . . can we get together?"

"Of course. Where are you?"

"At the Harris House, suite 1420."

Barry repeated it, motioning to a pad. Lobo wrote the address. Barry asked, "What's the phone number?" He repeated it when she gave it. "I'll come immediately."

"Thank you." She rang off.

Lobo said, "Why is she calling you? Is it possible it's a trap?"

"It could be but I don't think so."

"There are a dozen dead men in this case so far—"

"Why would Yashar want me dead?"

Lobo grinned. "You're the Establishment."

"You're getting your characters mixed. That's Freda Polk's line. Yashar wants to take over Kushka, doesn't he? That would make *him* super-Establishment." Barry rose and slipped into a sports jacket. "Besides, if

Elorith knows something, maybe we can use it. I can't afford to pass anything up."

Lobo sighed, "I suppose not."

"You'll have to stay here by the phone. If Tom calls back—or Frank—you know where I am."

Lobo grunted. "I'll call down for a cab."

The Harris House was a discreet and very elegant hotel that catered to those who demanded privacy. A maroon-coated doorman bowed Barry out of the cab, opened the lobby door for him, and resumed watching the street. A second man, with a scarlet coat and silver trimmings, lifted his eyebrows.

Barry said, "Miss Modan."

The man nodded, lifted a wall phone, and pushed an unnumbered button panel. He waited, staring at nothing. Then he turned slightly. "Your guest is here, Miss Modan." He nodded and replaced the receiver. "You may go up, sir. Suite 1420." He used a key fastened to his belt by a chain and unlocked a steel grill door. An elevator stood waiting.

At suite 1420 Elorith opened the door for Barry. She smiled, extending her hand. "I'm so glad you came." The smile was cool and her dark eyes unreadable. She wore a floor-length loose gown of deep blue, a cloth that winked in the somber light of the outer room. There was a heavy gold chain about her neck.

"You piqued my curiosity. How could I refuse?" He touched his lips to her hand gallantly and felt the warm shock as his flesh met hers. She withdrew her fingers gently and led the way to a living room.

The apartment was a perfect setting for Elorith's dark, brooding beauty. The room hinted at the East, lush draperies and a huge tapestry that looked vaguely Byzantine. There were curiously shaped lamps and a fine oriental on the floor. The coffee table was ivory and steel, the couches thick with pillows of gold, yellow, and blue.

Barry sat beside her on a couch, watching her light a cigarette with trembling fingers. He said, "You look terribly serious." Had something happened he hadn't heard about?

"I suppose I do." She glanced at him and pressed her lips together. "I—I've had news from my uncle that upsets me."

"I hope he's in good health."

"Oh yes." Elorith nodded quickly. "But there has been trouble."

Barry leaned back, taking a case from his pocket and extracting a cigarette. He moulded it in strong fingers. "We heard the news this morning about the ultimatum. All Americans must leave Kushka. Is that it?"

"That is part of it." Elorith smoked, looked at the end of the cigarette as if it had bit her, and crushed it out. "It is true the groups opposing my uncle the Shah have made threats. But they do not speak for Kushka." She glanced at Barry and away. "A military take-over is possible, I suppose. But not likely."

"Then it hasn't heppened yet?"

"No, it has not. I have been in communication with—" She broke off. She took a breath as though starting again. "When you and I talked last, I told you the Shah was in sympathy with the National Liberation Army's views." She shrugged. "And I too." She fumbled in a carved box for another cigarette. "Our country has been backward for too long, clinging to the old ways. We must make changes—but not this way."

"Not Yashar's way?"

"No. Never *his* way. The National Liberation Army—so-called—has apparently decided the time is ripe for them to strike. The trouble they are causing here in your country is proof of it. We believe either their views have changed from those they previously stated or that they were lying to us before. We no longer believe they are interested in peace."

Barry nodded. She meant the Shah and his government when she said "we."

Elorith continued, "Actually the National Liberation Army has been a political party in my country for several years. It has always advocated Kushka for its own people but in the past it has never been radical. Ali Yashar has divided the party and he leads a radical faction. He has changed everything in a short time."

Barry asked, "Have you met Yashar?"

"I am coming to that. Yashar's faction has men and arms in the towns of Kushka, ready to do whatever is necessary to gain their objectives. In the United States Yashar controls the stolen nerve gas." She looked away from him.

"Can the Shah deal with the militant faction in Kushka?"

"I pray he can. *He* is sure and the army is loyal to him. If trouble comes he will deal with it at once."

"Perhaps the Shah should take definite action now. The world only hears Yashar's threats—"

"He will act." She brought her gaze back to him. "I have come to realize that Yashar is a most dangerous man. I no longer think he is bluffing. He means to get what he wants and I fear he might be pushed into actually using the gas. He must be stopped."

So she had changed her opinion. How close to Yashar's organization was she? Elorith was young, not of her uncle's generation. She might have espoused Yashar's cause believing it good for Kushka, perhaps even going farther than she wished along that road. Now she had to pull back.

He said, "Do you know where Yashar is?"

She looked away, shaking her head. "No, I do not.

130

But I have friends in his organization. I hear many things." She glanced at him. "Such as the incident in Denver."

Barry's skin prickled. "Yashar was behind that?"

She nodded slightly. "He arranged it. Jeremiah Polk was too good not to use. The old man believed he was acting on God's will—he was sincere. But Yashar betrayed his faith and used Polk's zeal to demonstrate what could happen if the gas was loosed on an American city. Yashar wanted a panic as a warning of what could happen at any time and any place."

Elorith was holding herself firmly in check, her face pale. Her hands, twisted together in her lap, were the only signs of inner turmoil.

"After they used Polk, they killed him?"

She took a breath. "So he could not betray them. He had seen Ali Yashar himself."

"How do you know all this?"

"Through friends. Jeremiah Polk was told the tank contained only compressed air, nothing more except an odor-causing material. He was told to release the air in the tank and return to his trailer home."

"You are sure you don't know where Yashar is now?"

She shook her head, avoiding his eyes. "I do not know. It is a closely guarded secret. If I tried too hard to find out they might kill me."

"Are you guarded here?"

"Yes, there are two of my uncle's guards with me." She glanced toward the end of the room. "They are watching us now. I—I am perfectly safe, as long as I remain in this apartment."

"Tell me about Yashar. We have been able to learn very little about him."

Elorith nodded. "He was once an officer in the Shah's army. He was a very good soldier and a capable man. He helped lead the forces that overthrew the old regime and established my uncle in power—a rule that had been good for Kushka. Yashar was a faithful man who worked very hard for peace after the military action was over. He helped bring the feuding sheiks together. He was a good man, Barry. I do not know what has happened to cause the change in him. I still find it hard to believe—" She stopped short and composed herself again.

"You knew him well in Kushka?" He wondered how well.

She nodded slowly. "I thought once that I might—marry him." Her voice changed somewhat. "All that is over now."

"Do you know where the gas canisters are hidden?"

"No, only rumors. I was told once, in secret, that they are buried in Pennsylvania but I do not know where. It is a large state."

Barry worried his chin. Could Yashar have moved the remaining four canisters to Pennsylvania? It *was* possible, but he thought it unlikely. And, as she had said, it was a large state.

Elorith's hand reached out to touch Barry. "I have something to ask you . . ."

"What is it?"

"I have agreed to ask you but the decision is yours."

Barry blinked at her. "You have been asked by the NLA?"

"Yes. They want someone to act as intermediary, someone with your stature, and someone who is not in the government. Also, you have oil holdings in Kushka."

He sat back in surprise. "Yashar wants a meeting?"

She nodded. "He says his demands must be met. I think you know what they are. It is most important the five prisoners be released first." She glanced at him. "You realize I am only saying what I have been told."

Barry got up to pace the room. A meeting with the

mysterious Yashar? Very interesting. If there was any-thing he could do he would do it. He paused, looking at her. "You can arrange the meeting?"

"Yes. I am to call a number, then you will be con-tacted by telephone."

Yashar's deadline was almost up. Barry walked to a window and stared at the street below. Was Elorith telling the truth? Or was she really a member of the NLA, pretending to be shocked at Yashar's methods? That was possible, too. But the idea of a meeting sounded all right. If Yashar wanted Barry dead, this would be a clumsy way to arrange it. Barry went to the couch and sat down again. "All right. Have them phone me."

She smiled. "There is one more thing I want to show you."

"What?"

She reached for a square of paper that had been lying on the coffee table all the time he had been in the apart-ment. Picking it up, she turned it over and handed it to him. It was a photograph of four people. Barry studied it. One was Elorith, taken several years previously. The three others were men. He looked up at her.

She said, "Yashar is the man on the right."

Chapter Fourteen

Barry stared at the tiny image. Ali Yashar was a big man with black hair, a swarthy complextion, and a toothy smile. He was dressed in western garb, a dark suit and tie. The background of the photo was a mass of trees. It might have been taken anywhere.

"You may have the copy," Elorith said. "It is the only one I know of. Even in those days Yashar did not like to be photographed."

Barry put it away carefully.

She said, "He has a moustache now. The photograph may not do much good."

"It crystalizes things to see the enemy." Barry rose. "I'll stay at the hotel until I get the phone call."

Elorith saw him to the foor.

Lobo was astonished to hear of the possibility of a meeting. "You're not going?!" he growled.

"I have to. What better way to—"

"What better way to trap you! Why do they select *you*? There are dozens of oil companies dealing with Kushka. You think you can trust a man who has stolen five canisters of the most deadly—"

"He has to talk to someone."

Lobo sighed as if talking to a recalcitrant child. "It's too risky, Barry. You can't do it."

Barry lit a cigarette and dropped into the corner of a couch. He had considered the same possibilities, had the same doubts. But was there another choice? This was the first break, the first lead to Yashar himself. It might be the only one they'd get. If the man was unstable, he might convince himself that no one would deal with him, and release the gas.

Barry gave the photo to Lobo. "Cut everyone else

out of it and see that it gets distribution. Elorith said that he has a moustache now, maybe an artist could paint one in."

"It's not a very good photo," Lobo said, studying it. "It could cause more trouble than it's worth. I mean, through wrong identifications. Do you think that's the reason Elorith gave it to you?"

Barry shrugged. Lobo obviously did not trust Elorith Modan. Maybe he was right. The snapshot wasn't much and the man identified as Yashar did look like any of a great number of people. Barry said, "Have it sent out anyway. Let the police decide what to do with it."

Lobo nodded and put the photo into an envelope.

Barry said, "About the meeting, we'll take whatever precautions we can. Get Frank on the line. I want to be covered from the time I leave here."

Lobo looked at him. "That won't be easy if they're at all careful."

"They will be."

Lobo growled and sighed. "Okay, I know when I'm beat. But you're not going alone. Make sure they know I'm coming along."

Newsmen on TV kept up a steady stream of commentary and bulletins. The newspapers published reams of material about Kushka, the oil business, and the Middle East in general. Historical archives provided facts, such as Ali Yashar's participation in the overthrow of the old regime in Kushka, but no pictures. There were several artist's sketches of a man in flowing robes, with desert backgrounds, labeled Yashar. He looked like a million other gimlet-eyed Arab figures.

The United Council of Churches met in national conference and selected a delegation to meet with the President. The Secretary of State appeared in an unprecedented television appeal to the Kushka militants to negotiate in the name of humanity. Ali Yashar was implored to

135

contact the White House directly, to set up a meeting at the highest levels.

There had been no answer from Yashar.

There was an appeal from the President himself. "Let us talk like reasonable men . . ."

The five prisoners were still in jail.

The deadline was coming closer.

Barry reached for the telephone himself. He let it ring twice. "Hello."

Elorith Modan sounded excited. "He agreed, Barry. The meeting is set."

Barry turned, seeing Lobo pick up the extension. "When will it be?"

"Immediately. He's sending a car for you. It will be in front of your hotel in exactly an hour."

"In an hour?!"

"Yashar insists on taking precautions so you will not know where you are being driven. He is afraid of a trap."

"*He* is afraid?! I'm the one taking the chances." Barry could see Lobo frowning.

"Barry, he's paranoid. Please put up with him."

"All right, but I'm taking my secretary with me. Lloyd Fenner. You met him at the party."

She paused. "You are to be alone."

"Fenner knows the details of our Kushkan holdings and he knows details of a great many things. I need him there. Arrange it, Elorith."

Her voice sounded doubtful. "I—I don't know. I will try." She sighed. "Be ready in an hour. The car will be on time. The driver will ask for you by name and he knows what you look like." She stopped and for a moment Barry thought the conversation was over. Then in almost a whisper she said, "Be careful, Barry, and good luck." The line clicked dead.

Lobo asked, "Will Yashar buy it?"

Barry frowned, replacing the receiver. "If any part of this is on the up and up I don't see why not. They'll search us, of course."

"But probably only for weapons. Let me show you what Frank had sent over." Lobo went for a box and returned. He opened the box and laid out two minute metal objects that looked like shirt buttons. "Homing devices," he said.

Barry examined one. It had a snap on the back so it could be fastened in place quickly. He watched Lobo snip off one of his own shirt buttons and fasten the device in place of it. He glanced up with a grin, "Let's hope these things work."

Barry deftly clipped the button on his own shirt. The devices might work fine but they'd be little help if the two of them got into serious trouble. Frank Trask would be able to find their bodies later—that was about it.

They were waiting downstairs when the black limousine pulled to the curb. The doorman leaned to the window as it whispered down. He spoke to someone inside then opened the rear door and nodded to Barry. "Your car, sir."

There were two men in the car, the driver and a man who sat on one of the rear jump seats. He was unsmiling as Barry and Lobo slid in. As soon as the rear door slammed the car was underway. Barry studied the man opposite. Dark and olive-slinned, he looked Mid-Eastern. The man did not show a pistol but Barry was sure it would take only the slightest suspicious move on his or Lobo's part to bring one out. The man said nothing and did not take his eyes off them.

The limousine left the city on the River Road heading northwest. The driver made good time in the gathering darkness. Well out of the city the man on the jump seat reached into his pocket and pulled out two black masks. "Put these on," he said in a throaty, accented voice. He gave them each a mask and watched as Barry and Lobo adjusted them.

Barry settled back, forcing himself to relax. He was not surprised at the masks. Were they headed toward Pennsylvania? Elorith had admitted the canisters might be cached there. He heard the whisper of cloth and knew the guard had drawn curtains over the windows as an additional precaution. Their isolation was complete. He and Lobo could do nothing but wait, even if the homing devices worked.

He tried to judge time but it was difficult in the silent darkness. Barry was sure the car had covered enough miles and had made enough turnings to have crossed into Pennsylvania. They passed through a town that might have been Frederick or Hagerstown but the driver might have doubled back, taking them through a circular course—it was impossible to tell. They could be back in Washington, only blocks from where they started.

Then the car left the highway and bumped along a rutted road, slowing to a crawl. Barry could hear the swish of weeds and the tiny sounds of pebbles and dirt flung against the underside. They were on a dirt road, no doubt about it. So they were not in a city. The car's engine labored as they climbed a hill. Finally, after another twenty minutes on the secondary road, the car slowed, turned and came to a stop. The driver cut the engine and got out.

The door next to Barry opened and he felt the rush of cool night air. He could hear the steady thrum of crickets and smell the freshness of fields and pines.

"Come along," the throaty voice said. A hand tugged at Barry's sleeve.

He got out, feeling steely fingers on his arm propelling him forward. He smelled the heavy odors of fertilizer and plowed earth. They must be near a farm. The fingers dug into his arm and he had to force himself not to harden his muscles against them. He heard the sounds as Lobo slid from the car behind him. The car door slammed.

"This way," Throaty Voice said. They walked over a gritty stretch of ground. A door squeaked ahead of them.

"Up steps," the voice said.

Barry felt for them, mounted five wooden steps, and crossed a narrow porch. Warm, dry air from inside the house met him. He smelled the sweet aroma of Turkish tobacco.

Throaty Voice said something in a staccato burst, a language Barry did not understand, and another voice answered. Barry was shoved past someone. His heels clicked on a hard linoleum floor. Food odors were strong.

Behind him, a sharp grunt died in a moan.

Barry wheeled, "Lobo?" Arms gripped him and yanked him around. He said loudly, "Lobo—what happened?"

"You were told to come alone."

Barry struggled for a second. Two men held him. "If anything's happened to—"

"Silence. We will do the talking. Your friend is not hurt."

There was a mumble of voices; shoes scuffled on the floor. Barry ground his teeth. Had they taken Lobo into another room? He heard a door slam and someone came back.

"All right, take him in there." The voice said, "Ali Yashar wants to see you alone."

Barry was led down a hallway. The guard said something softly, a door opened. Barry was brought into a room that smelled of incense. Someone snatched off the blindfold.

It was a room almost bare of furniture, a large, square room that might have been a bedroom at one time. An ancient stone fireplace at one end of the room took up most of the wall. A high wardrobe closet in rubbed walnut stood against another. A bare, dark table stood in the center of the room. There were several straight-backed chairs and a bit of dark carpet on the floor.

A big, swarthy man sat at the table, staring at Barry.

"I am Ali Yashar, Mr. Hewes-Bradford." His voice was deep and harsh, seeming to rumble in his chest. "I have heard much about you."

Barry nodded and studied the man's dark face in the dim light. There was only a shaded lamp and the leaping flames in the fireplace. Yashar did not in the least resemble the man of Elorith's photograph. He was years older and heavier and wore a heavy moustache. Elorith had given him a useless bit of information. This man was an imposing figure with wide shoulders, muscular arms, and an air of authority.

"I've heard quite a bit about you, too, lately," Barry said.

Yashar laughed, a deep booming rumble that exploded from his chest and echoed in the room. "Yes, the entire world hears of Ali Yashar now." The laughter quickly died and Yashar resumed his scowl. "And the world listens now."

"The man I brought with me," Barry said. "Have you harmed him?"

Yashar shrugged. "He will recover. My business is with you."

"He's part of my business." Barry was icy, containing his anger by rigid control. "What happened to him?"

Yashar shrugged, looking up almost curiously. "He suffered a small reverse. He is in another room under guard. Do not concern yourself with him."

"I assure you—"

"We are wasting time." Yashar snapped his fingers in

140

annoyance. He pointed to a chair.

The man of the jump seat quickly brought a chair and placed it across the table from Yashar, then looked at Barry. Barry sat, both hands on the table. The man retreated to the door but did not go out.

"All right," Barry said. "What is it?"

"You will go to your President and convince him that I exist."

Barry almost smiled. There had been commentators on the air speculating that Ali Yashar was only a name, since they could find no evidence that such a man lived. Apparently they had pricked the man's ego. He nodded.

"You will convince him and his ministers that I exist and that I am serious and that my demands must be met."

"Am I to act as a go-between?"

Yashar shrugged again. "You will tell them to accept my demands. They have less than twenty-four hours before the deadline. I picked you, Mr. Hewes-Bradford, because of your extensive holdings in Kushka. Your company has been in my country a long time. We have never met but I have heard much about you."

Barry nodded. "You plan to depose the Shah?"

Yashar leaned forward. "I plan to do many things, Mr. Hewes-Bradford, in the proper time. You will do this for me—if you want to keep your oil."

"You will allow my company to operate?"

"That may be."

Barry smiled thinly. "And who will you sell Kushkan oil to if you close off world markets?"

Yashar scowled. "I did not bring you here to be a schoolmaster. You will carry my demands to your President—or you will be sent away. You saw what happened in Denver. It will happen in Washington, only next time it will be the poison gas."

Barry stared at the man across the table. "I can carry your threats to—"

Yashar screamed suddenly. He pounded the table, half rising from the chair. "They are not threats!" Blood suffused his face and he pointed a thick finger at Barry. "I will do this thing if you force me. It will be your fault, not mine."

Barry said, "I will carry your demands. But they will ask me something else."

"What is that?"

"The President will want to know what assurances he has that the canisters of gas will be returned unused."

"You have my word."

Barry paused. His gaze bored into the black pools under Yashar's thick brows. The other's eyes were like obsidian, opaque and unreadable. He said, "They will require something more concrete, Mr. Yashar."

Yashar pounded the table again, brows contracted, face scowling. "My word is good enough! Make no mistake, I will do as I say!"

Barry shrugged. "Then I can promise nothing."

Yashar rose abruptly and signaled the man at the door. "Take them back." He turned to the fire and put out his hands as if to warm them. The meeting was over.

Barry went to the door and the guard handed him the blindfold.

Behind him, Yashar said, "Carry my words to your President, Hewes-Bradford. I mean what I say."

Barry nodded, saying nothing. He put on the blindfold. He was led back through the house and down the back steps. The outside air seemed colder. He got into the car, pushing against a slumped body. "Lobo?"

The guard slid into the car and folded down the jump seat. "He will be all right soon."

The limousine moved, backed, then rolled out of the farmyard and onto the dirt road again. Barry sighed and settled back. One thing he was sure of. Yashar would never turn over the gas canisters, even if his demands were met. A blackmailer always had other demands.

Chapter Fifteen

Dawn feathered the distant horizon with pale gray as the boat's engine sputtered into life. It settled into a throbbing rhythm that made the small craft vibrate. The man at the wheel frowned nervously at the cargo and at the two men standing in the stern.

Ceri Vilgot didn't like the job. He didn't like it one damned bit. Yet he knew that if he did protest it would be as the bawling of a calf on the hillside. No one would listen. He would be forced to run the boat for them, maybe even at gun point. It was too late to back out now.

He silently cursed the fate that had thrown him in with Ali Yashar's Army of Liberation. How he regretted it! He was having second thoughts. The entire idea had sounded fine at first, a magnificent gesture that would help bring the people of Kushka their rights in the hard world. One had to fight for his own, but Ceri was afraid of Yashar. The man had changed so. No longer did Yashar seem to care about ordinary things. The man was caught up in the power madness. Nothing mattered to Yashar but power. Nothing.

Abruptly Ceri forced his thoughts away from the black past and the many deaths that marred Yashar's actions. It was better not to think of those things. Not when the boat's cargo was so deadly.

In the stern was a dinghy, secured on a specially designed frame. It could slide into the water in a mo-

143

ment, when they were far enough off shore. On the dinghy was a tank of gas. Ceri felt the prickle of sweat between his shoulder blades, despite the cold of the morning breeze. Suppose something should go wrong? If the timer on the tank malfunctioned, clicked off before the cursed thing was afloat and safely away from the boat—it was not a pleasant thought. They would all be dead. With no warning.

He steered the boat through the channel, more carefully than he had ever done. The Virginia shore was vague and misty in the darkness behind them. He could see a few lights, almost obscured. He knew no one could see them from shore.

One of the men in the stern, hunched under a damp slicker, came forward and leaned into the cabin.

"How long will it take?"

Ceri made a face. "An hour, maybe a little longer. We have to go slow in the fog. Besides, this boat was not made for racing."

"It smells like a fish trap."

"It is a fishing boat."

The man grunted. "When can we smoke?"

"In another fifteen minutes."

The man shuddered and slapped his arms. "It's colder than a camel's stare. Are you sure that thing on the dinghy is safe?"

"I fastened it myself," Ceri said. "I am sure it will not come free. The timer is something else."

"We double-checked it. There's nothing to worry about."

Ceri was silent, peering through the mist-covered windscreen at the dull sea. His two passengers *were* worried. He detected the note of anxiety in Stack's voice. And Mardo, sitting by the dinghy, was staring at the tank.

It would be light soon but the sky would be overcast. It was going to be a dismal day.

Ceri sighed heavily. Yes, it was going to be a very dismal day. He cursed his lot in life, the fates that had brought him to this smelly fishing boat.

Lobo sat with eyes closed. His head still throbbed where he'd been clouted last night. Walking behind Barry into the farmhouse, propelled by unseen hands, he had been felled. He wasn't sure he remembered the blow but the next thing he'd known he was coming to with a terrible pain, groggy and sick. He was back in the moving limousine. Then, as he'd struggled with consciousness, Barry had told him to relax. Barry's voice had warned him it was not a time for talking.

So he'd nursed the headache and nausea for the remainder of the ride. They had removed the masks when the car reached the city, and they'd been let out at the Carillon Hotel.

Barry had filled him in about the events at the farmhouse, then called Frank Trask.

"We're back safe, Frank. What about your end?"

Frank reported that the homing devices had worked perfectly. "Our men were both in front of and behind you the whole way, Barry. You were taken to a farm in Pennsylvania, just over the Maryland border. One of our men got close enough to the house to watch for cars after you left. Yashar and his men cleared out immediately."

"How about the house?"

"Owned by a couple who are visiting out of the state. After the cars left we closed in and found a caretaker tied up on a bed in the basement. He didn't know a thing."

Barry grunted.

Frank said, "We followed them to Philadelphia. But unfortunately lost them. Yashar engaged in evasive tactics, like he thought he might be tailed."

"You're still trying to find him?"

"Affirmative. Every available man is on it. What happened at the meeting?"

Barry told him. "I've got to call the White House, Frank. Maybe I should go see the President myself, though I haven't got a damn new thing to say."

"I'll arrange it if you like."

"Good." Barry talked a few more minutes but Lobo tuned it out. Yashar's goons could have pushed him into another room instead of hitting him. If he got his hands on one of them—

Barry asked, "How is it now?"

"I'll survive." Lobo sat up, wincing. His head felt like a pillow with a jelly center. He switched on a TV set to check on the news.

The country was drifting back to near normal. No new threats had shaken it. Violent protests had tailed off; the marchers had packed up for the most part. The nation was in a state of uneasy waiting. Repeated announcements from the authorities reiterated that negotiations were progressing.

The news bulletin was flashed on the air a few minutes before noon.

"Nineteen persons, three of them children, have died of nerve gas! Dozens of people have been felled on the streets of Templeton, Virginia, a small coastal town. In addition to the nineteen known dead, scores have suffered some effects of the gas and have been rushed to the Naval Hospital in Norfolk. It is not known at this time if their conditions are serious. Authorities in Templeton theorize that the deadly gas was blown ashore from a vessel at sea. A steady breeze was blowing according to . . ."

Barry began to swear. Lobo said, "Jesus! Another one! The bastard didn't wait."

"A later report has just come in. It has been definitely determined that the gas was not released in the town itself but from a boat offshore and carried to land by a shift of wind coming as a result of an approaching tropical storm.

"Coast Guard and Navy ships and planes have been deployed to search for the source of the poison gas.

"In the meantime every available precaution is being taken to prevent further deaths. People along the entire middle-Eastern seaboard are being evacuated. Emergency aid stations are being set up to care for the scores of persons injured in the mass panic that has erupted in several cities. Officials and police ask your cooperation in this dire emergency. Unless you live in one of the evacuated communities, do not travel. Food and clothing are desperately needed. Collection points are being set up. There is no official estimate of the time required to determine the scope of the gas tragedy. . . . "

Lobo said, "So much for Yashar's promises."

Barry sat back, swearing softly. "I don't understand it." He shook his head, staring at the TV screen. "Why wouldn't he at least wait until the deadline?! He can't be stupid enough to think anyone will believe him after this!"

The phone rang and Lobo answered it. He handed it over. "Frank's on the line."

Barry listened to his Chief of Staff for a moment. "Okay, Frank, let's let it hang till we hear from Yashar—if we do. We have to assume now that he's off the deep end. Any persuasion on my part would be laughed at, I think." He paused, listening. "Yes, I agree. And this thing in Templeton makes it worse. We

147

have to assume he will release the gas at any time. All bets are off."

Lobo raked fingers through his hair, wincing as they touched the sore spot he had momentarily forgotten.

Barry hung up. "Frank agrees. There's no point in trying to influence the White House on anything now. Yashar has just ended the game."

Lobo said, "I think you should get out of Washington."

Barry shook his head, staring at the screen. An announcer was using a pointer to trace the extent of the gas tragedy on a map. "Not while there's a chance. Yashar knows where to find me." He smiled thinly. "Besides, do we have any assurance that Hewesridge is any safer than Washington?" He shrugged eloquently. "The way I see it, this may be the safest spot in the entire country after all."

"How so?"

"First of all, the five prisoners Yashar is so desperate to free are here. Second, if Yashar hopes to work out a deal with the government, he has to leave enough of it intact to work with."

Lobo nodded. That *was* a point.

Ceri Vilgot was sweating. The news of the deadly gas that had felled residents of a small town only a hundred miles behind them had unnerved him.

He'd had a feeling all along that something would go wrong! It was a miracle they were still alive. He'd had no faith in the timer from the beginning . . . and he'd told Mardo that it looked too old and unreliable. The thing had gone off prematurely, releasing the nerve gas before Yashar's deadline. Before Ceri and the others were safely away!

According to the radio, all the roads were jammed with cars and trucks as people fled the coast in panic.

Suppose the wind shifted? Was there enough gas in the small canister to reach this far? He had no idea how much gas it took to spread over a large area. No one among them had. Ceri's mouth was dry.

They had run the boat ashore far up the coast, upwind of the storm that was moving in. Stack had a car hidden and they got in, all of them pale and shaking. It was enough to unnerve the strongest. A man could suddenly fall down and be dead in seconds! Stack drove, gunning the car toward the highway, then slamming on the brakes when they got near.

The highway was jammed. Stack swore in two languages. Mardo said, "Where's the goddamn map?"

They found a secondary road, busy with traffic, but not like the main highway. They went west and north, trying to skirt the heaviest traffic, driving hard to circle back toward Pennsylvania. The farther they got from the coast, the easier it went. Police and troops were everywhere, trying to keep traffic moving, pulling stalled cars out, putting up signs.

Ceri sat, smoking too much, staring at the white faces in other cars. It had been foolish and stupid to attempt any work with the gas canisters without Josef. Draggett was the only one of them skilled enough to transfer the deadly gas from the Army canister to the smaller one they had used at sea. Josef would have made sure the timer was not defective—would not go off nine hours early!

But Josef was still in jail with the others. Would the Americans release him now?

Ceri was afraid. What if his own part in this became known? What if he was caught? The people were in a mood to hang him without waiting for a trial. He wiped a hand across his sweating face. How he wished he were out of this! But Stack and Mardo were in charge and they were heading back to Yashar's hideout.

Yes, he wished he were out of this. Could he get

away? Ceri sat up in the back of the car, staring at the passing countryside. Stack had taken a secondary road, black asphalt, narrow, with weeds and wire fences straggling along both sides. There were dozens of other cars on the road but not bumper to bumper. Maybe he could slip away if Stack halted the car somewhere. Neither Stack nor Mardo cared about him. Maybe he could slip away unnoticed.

Sweat dampened the shirt between his shoulder blades. He was a small man, thin and not nearly as strong as either of his companions. And he was unarmed. Both Stack and Mardo had pistols. Ceri had seen them. He had been part of the mission only because of his knowledge of boats.

Mardo was sitting beside Stack in the front seat, with the map on his lap. He had made a line on the map with a pencil and was guiding Stack. "Take a right here, turn left there . . ."

In the rear seat, Ceri began to formulate a plan. If he got away from them he could lose himself somewhere. There were plenty of places. He could be a handy man or get a job at any of a dozen things . . . he was good with tools. There weren't enough of Yashar's men to really search for him. But why should Yashar care?

He stared out. They were on the crest of a ridge, a narrow black ribbon that wound over the low hills. Tall pines, almost blue in the hazy morning light, towered above them on the left. To the right, the hill fell away sharply to the valley below. Ceri moved close to the right-hand side of the car, examining the slope and the valley. There were trees down there, thick and misty. The slope was steep and, as he caught glimpses of it ahead, looked grassy.

He glanced at the two in the front seat. Stack was intent on driving and listening to the radio which was repeating almost monotonously a recitation of the past events. Mardo was bent over the map, smoking one cigarette after another. Neither of them had spoken to him or even glanced in his direction for a long time.

Ceri slipped his hand over the door handle and worked it up slowly. The weight of the door was heavy and he wedged his foot against it. Ahead, he saw a dip, then another upgrade. The car was picking up speed. He took a long breath. Yes, this was his only chance. His fingers tightened on the door handle until they hurt.

"In about five miles there's another junction," Mardo said. "If there's not much traffic we can bear right again."

The engine began to roar as Stack gunned it for the upward surge. Ceri paused, gritted his teeth, then shoved suddenly against the door. He threw himself outward, pushing off with his feet. He dived into the air, seeing the weeds and grass whirling by so close to his eyes. He heard a shout.

He hit the dirt at the side of the road. Pain slashed through him. His head hurt. He was rolling. He dimly heard the sound of brakes as the car skidded. He curled into a ball, rolling and bouncing with dizzying speed. The hillside was littered with hard clumps of grass and rocks. Someone was shouting, yelling his name. What a long way down!

He fell into a ditch, arms and legs splayed, head throbbing with pain. He lay still for seconds, wondering how badly he was hurt. Were any limbs broken? His arms were all right. He moved his legs, and sat up . . . dizzy. He stared back up the hill. It looked a mile to the top. Had he come down that?!

"There he is!" Mardo's voice was clear.

Ceri stared numbly as he saw Mardo point at him. Then he realized Mardo had a gun. A shot spanged into the dirt near him. Ceri scrambled up, flinging himself into the trees and brush. A second and a third shot came, rapping into tree trunks, ricocheting into the sky.

151

He fell full length, sprawling in the wet grass. He hurt all over. His heart was pounding as if to tear itself out of his chest. Was this any way to die?

The announcer interrupted the coverage of the events in Templeton and the erupting riots in Washington with a bulletin. Another communication had been received from the National Liberation Army. The small town in Virginia could just have well been Washington, D.C., or New York City. The United States must release the Kushkan prisoners immediately. The five men were to be driven to a contact point that would be phoned to the FBI. They were to be set free, all roads cleared, and the men provided with a car. If they were followed, a canister of gas, already in position in a large eastern city, would be released. There would be no further warnings. Refusal to cooperate on the part of the United States government would be considered an act of war by the Kushkans.

Barry held a fresh cigarette to the glowing tip of the stub in his mouth. It was madness, sheer madness! What the hell had happened to push Yashar into this?

He blew smoke, pacing the confines of the large room of the suite. "Get me Elorith Modan on the phone, Lobo."

Would she know anything? Was her uncle still in control of his government or had the Liberationists swarmed the palace by now? Several minutes later, Lobo handed him the phone.

"Barry, I'm so glad to hear from you——" Elorith sounded breathless and as if she had been crying.

"What the devil is Yashar up to, Elorith? I thought we'd made a bargain."

"Yes, I know. I mean I don't know. I acted in the belief he was truly trying to come to terms. Oh, Barry, I am sick with grief over the terrible needless deaths." She broke off with a sob.

152

Barry knew he should be suspicious. It was quite possible that she was with the Liberationists all the way. She could have set Barry up last night; Yashar might still have some tricks up his sleeve that were not obvious.

Yet he believed her. "Have you been in contact with your uncle?" he asked.

She took a deep breath and her voice was controlled when she spoke again. "Yes. He is preparing a public announcement. He no longer believes Yashar and his party work for the good of the people. He is horrified at the gas incidents. He will issue a statement denouncing the militants completely. He will join with the United States and all the countries of the free world in wanting to see them stopped as soon as possible. Barry : . . I wish there was something I could do to help."

"Get me to Yashar again. I want to talk to him."

She caught her breath. "No—"

"It's the only chance, Elorith. Nineteen people died today because of Yashar. I have to try."

There was a short silence. "But I don't know where he is. I swear it, Barry. Don't you think I would tell you if I knew?"

"You found him yesterday. Do it again."

"What good—?"

"Elorith, he's a madman. If he thinks there's no chance at all of his demands being met, what will he do? It could be disastrous."

"But—"

"If he won't meet with me, then let him say who he wants in my place. He can decide the time. I'll go anywhere at all."

"Barry, you have no official status!"

"Get to Yashar, Elorith. I'll get some official clout. Most important, Yashar must feel the government wants to deal with him. If nothing else, get him to call the White House!"

153

She sounded pushed into a corner. "All right, I'll try. But I'm not sure I can—"

"You've got to try."

She sighed, "Yes . . ."

When she hung up, Barry shook his head at Lobo. It did not ease his mind to have to depend on Elorith.

The phone rang a number of times in the next hour but Elorith did not call back. Franklin Trask reported that Tom Radley had been reassigned from Denver and with another man had a lead on the limo which had taken Barry and Lobo to the farmhouse.

"It came from an airport rental-service in Wilmington, Barry. I'll keep you posted."

An agent hired by Lobo reported that Freda Polk had taken a car from a spot near the Monument Grounds and been driven across Washington, changed cars, and had been lost.

"She must have changed into man's clothes in the car," the agent said on the phone. "We weren't ready for the second switch. She left us holding the sack."

"Damn," Lobo growled.

Chapter Sixteen

Tom Radley called twenty minutes later. "Let me talk to Barry . . ."

When Barry lifted the receiver, Tom said, "I'm in Baltimore, boss. I'm chasing down the limo. It was rented by a man named Stefan Durak, with a Delaware license. I've checked the license and it's valid. Durak is a machinist who hasn't been out of the house for a month."

"What?"

Tom's voice held a chuckle. "He's in a wheelchair with a broken leg. Full cast from the hip down. You couldn't get him up with anything less than a block and tackle."

"Then someone else used the limousine."

"Exactly. I think I know who."

"Who?" Lobo growled on the extension.

"His wife's brother. Guy named Sonny Pringle."

"Pringle?!" Barry said. "How old is he?"

"Just a kid. Durak says the guy is a no-good bum who never worked a day in his life. Long-hair, radical—Durak says he hasn't seen the kid in a week or so. Doesn't care much if he ever does again."

"Do you have an address on him?"

Tom chuckled again. "That's what I'm doing in Baltimore. According to Durak the kid is staying with a girlfriend outside of town. Durak intercepted a letter. It cost you twenty bucks for the address."

"Worth it," Barry said, reaching for a road map. This elusive Sonny Pringle *might* be able to lead them to Yashar. "We're leaving here in five minutes, Tom." He saw Lobo hang up and use another phone to call for a car. He arranged a meeting place with Tom, called Elorith, and gave her Trask's number at Hewesridge. Elorith had not yet been able to contact Yashar. He urged her to try harder. Barry and Lobo stopped to attach the electronic homing devices Frank had provided. "Insurance," Barry said, and they went down to the car.

They took Route 29, a divided highway, out of Washington. Tom Radley would meet them on the eastern outskirts of a small town called Bayard.

Lobo had rented a Plymouth and Barry drove it fast. They left 29, turned west onto a busy interstate highway and pulled into a supermarket parking lot at the edge of Bayard. Tom Radley was there, reading a newspaper in a small Chevy. He waved, left the Chevy, and came over to slide into the back of the Plymouth.

He took up the conversation as though they had left it only moments ago. "Durak says the only one who could have used the limo was Sonny. His wife drives but she's got a VW. Sonny swiped Durak's license, rented the limo with it, and managed to return the license without Durak seeing him. Sonny's the only other guy with a key to the house."

"You mean it had to be him," Lobo said.

"Right. And that's the way it is. It *had* to be him." Tom produced a map, and unfolded it. "This's the address, 650 Hayden Street." He tapped the paper with his finger. "I drove by it a half hour ago but nothing stirring. It's an old house on an old street." He looked at Barry.

Barry said, "There's only three of us. If we try to pick him up and miss—" He shrugged.

"That leaves two choices," Lobo said quickly.

"Either we get more men in a hurry and do it ourselves or we turn it over to the authorities."

Barry turned the ignition key. "I'd like to see the house first. Which way, Tom?" He got directions and drove slowly. "Lobo, call Frank and get a run-down on the Pringle kid. If he's a relative of the Pringle we already know about—"

"Okay, boss."

They let Lobo out at the nearest phone booth and went on another street to Hayden. As Tom had said, it was a rundown neighborhood with old, two-story houses, many needing paint. There were maples along the street and a number of shabby, parked cars.

But the car in front of number 650 was much newer. It was a robin's egg blue Thunderbird. Barry glanced at the brown house with its screen door and old-fashioned sconces. They went by without slowing, turned the next corner, and made a U in the middle of the next block. Barry eased the Plymouth back to the corner and parked where they could see the house from the car.

Tom jotted down the number of the Thunderbird's plates. "Wish we had a two-way radio."

Barry lit a cigarette, staring at the old house. The thing to do was call in the FBI, let them take over. If young Pringle had anything to impart they'd get it out of him. Sonny could be a very important witness. If he *had* rented the limo, he must be close to the men around Yashar. It was too important a lead to take a chance on. Yashar had already lost Barry's men once and Sonny Pringle might take them right to Yashar, if they were lucky. With so little time left, the smart thing to do was to call in the FBI.

Barry made up his mind. "Let's go back to the phone."

He reached for the ignition key and Tom said, "Wait—"

The screen door of the house they were watching

157

opened and a man came out. Tom said, "That's Sonny."

Barry saw a dark-haired young man dressed in dark pants and a brown jacket. He was talking with someone inside the screened porch. In a moment he waved and went out to the Thunderbird at the curb. Barry switched on the ignition as he saw smoke puff from the blue car's tailpipes. "We'll follow," he said.

He eased the car around the corner. The blue Ford was well down the block, slowing to make a left. Tom said, "He's going to the highway."

The blue car was turning left onto the interstate when they halted to pick up Lobo. For a few minutes the car was out of sight ahead of them. Barry floored the gas pedal as Tom explained what they were doing. "What'd you learn?"

"Sonny is Terrance Pringle's younger brother. Terrance is the guy who owns the garage," Lobo told them. "Sonny is a real bad cat. Juvenile stuff all his life, stealing radios and so on, joyriding—you know the bit. Frank's men didn't concentrate on him. They'll do it now. I gave Frank this address. Where do you think he's headed?"

Barry said, "Don't know." He glanced at them, "Maybe into Pennsylvania."

"There he is," Tom said, peering ahead. "Over in the fast lane. He's staying on the interstate for a while . . ."

Barry pulled into the fast lane, five cars behind the Thunderbird.

They stayed behind the blue car for an hour, crossing into Pennsylvania. Sonny moved off the interstate at Kester and went west on a state highway, maintaining a steady speed. They followed for another hour. At Hamilburg, Sonny eased off the highway and went north.

It was a narrow macadam road with little traffic.

Barry had to drop far behind to avoid detection. They went through a number of towns; in the fourth one, they lost sight of the blue Thunderbird. It was late afternoon and would soon be dark. If they didn't pick up the trail quickly, it would be too late.

Tom spotted the car in a gas station as they went past. It was a huge relief; they hadn't lost him. Barry pulled up a few miles out of town and let the Thunderbird go past again. They were able to keep the car in view better because of the hills.

From a slight ridge they saw the Thunderbird turn off the highway several miles ahead. The car went to the right on a dirt road, raising a plume of dust that was easy to spot.

"Dumb kid doesn't know enough to slow down," Tom commented.

Barry made a right on the same road and slowed to a crawl. He said a silent prayer for the shadows that were beginning to droop across the road as heavy clouds hid the sun. They were in for a storm. How far was Sonny going?

Barry had no doubts that Sonny was heading for Yashar's hideout. Why else would the man come into this sparsely settled district? It was unfortunate the close chase had prevented Barry from sending for reinforcements. It would feel good to know the FBI was close behind instead of only the three of them heading into this unknown situation. From now on they would have to play it by ear.

They saw evidence of abandoned coal diggings and it crossed Barry's mind for the first time that a deep mine might be the perfect hiding place for the canister of gas.

Tom said, "An abandoned coal mine! Why didn't we think of it before?"

Ceri Vilgot made his way across country, walking steadily, keeping to the trees. He could have made better time by crossing open fields but he was afraid to. Stack and Mardo would try to hunt him down; they were not stupid. And they would find him if he was careless.

But he had many things in his favor, Ceri knew. It was a large countryside, mostly farming, now that he was in the valley, and there were few roads.

Ceri turned south, in the opposite direction from the one they had been traveling. For miles he paralleled the range of hills. He saw many cars in the distance but he was far enough away from the road to stay out of sight.

Toward evening he entered the small town of Stillton. He walked the length of the town seeing nothing of his enemies. In a cafe next to a gas station he had a meal; then he hitched a ride to the next town.

He got several rides, reaching Washington in the middle of the next morning, unshaven and tired. At a phone booth he called Elorith Modan. He had some trouble getting through to her, but the words, "I was a friend of Yashar's," finally did the trick. He told Elorith his name and explained what had happened.

She sent a car for him.

Her first question when she saw him was, "What do you want of me?"

Ceri smiled nervously. "Money."

"In exchange for what?"

Ceri looked around. They were alone in a very plush sitting room. But anyone could be listening—he hesitated.

Elorith said, "You are among friends. What can you tell me of Yashar?"

"Are you Yashar's friend?"

She shook her head. "No longer."

"And you will give me money—and help me get away from Yashar?"

"I promise," Elorith said.

"Get me a large map then," Ceri Vilgot said. "I will show you where all the canisters are hidden."

They lost sight of Pringle's car again. The dirt road, winding into the hills, became almost impossible to follow and not risk coming upon him without warning. Barry maneuvered the Plymouth off the road and switched off the engine. They went on foot, walking in single file.

They came to a cluster of vacant houses and approached them warily. There were several trash heaps, a rusting automobile. It was an abandoned coal town. A few leafless trees threaded upward into the darkening sky. Barry could smell coal dust in the air.

They went on, staying at the side of the road and pausing often to listen for sounds ahead of them. When they saw the first glimmer of light, Barry motioned them to come together. "We'll have to watch for guards if we're getting close."

Radley said, "Let me go have a look—I'm an old country boy." He faded into the gloom immediately.

Lobo said, "If this *is* Yashar's hideout, what do we do next?"

"I wish I knew. It looks like an abandoned mine. If he's down in it, that's one thing but there may be another road out on the other side of the hill. I'd say our best bet is to try to find out if Yashar or the gas is here, then get the authorities on it. They can deploy enough men—"

"Suppose Yashar uses the nerve gas?"

Barry paused. That was always a big risk. He looked up as he felt the first feathery drops of rain. He said, "If Yashar is in the mine he won't risk using the gas here. It'll kill him just as easily as anyone else."

"Unless he can protect himself from it. He may be well-equipped with gas masks, oxygen—anything he needs."

Tom slipped soundlessly back beside them. "It's an old mine, obviously shut down a long time. The light is in some kind of a shed off to the left of the mine entrance. I couldn't see how many men there are but there's more than one. I heard voices. The Thunderbird and a truck are parked nearby."

"Any guards along the road?"

Tom pushed at his glasses. "Didn't see any, but there are half a dozen places a guy could stay out of sight. The rain may keep them inside."

"Would it be possible to get the canisters down into the mine?" Lobo asked.

Barry nodded. "They'd have to put the elevator back in working condition. My guess is Yashar picked this spot well in advance. He'd have had plenty of time to make sure everything was ready when the cylinders arrived." Barry glanced in the direction of the faint light. It was difficult to see now with the curtain of rain misting the hillside. "There are dozens of old mines like this around the state. This one's most likely a vertical shaft, maybe a hundred and sixty or seventy feet deep. The main gallery would be the most likely place for Yashar to use."

Radley said, "You sound like you know something about coal mines, Barry."

"I was brought up in Pennsylvania. My father had extensive mineral holdings around these parts. I've been in mines several times myself, and I remember some of the mine disasters that helped close old mines like this one. There probably wasn't enough coal left here for the company to spend money bringing the mine up to safety standards when the union got tough. They probably had a number of roof-falls and gas pockets, maybe even lost some men. If the guards are inside the shed, it's a break for us. They may not be near the shaft itself. Let's have a look."

They avoided the road as much as possible, cutting

162

along the edge of the trees some fifty yards back. There might be a guard; it was better to play it safe. The ground sloped upward at a sharp angle and the gray dust of slag piles formed a thick crust under their feet. Radley took the lead, retracing his earlier route. The hillside was quiet except for the whisper of the rain in the trees. It was hard to believe that death and destruction might lie so close at hand.

Then they were at the clearing. The entrance to the mine was a huge barren spot on the side of the hill. Remnants of rusting machinery were scattered about; a pile of timber posts had toppled near the entrance to the mine. The gaping doors and windows of the mine entrance shack showed that the machinery had been removed and some of the railroad tracks pulled up. About thirty feet to the left, a small shed had been repaired in a make-shift fashion with boards and tin; the pale light inside seemed to come from a lantern. An occasional murmur of voices drifted from inside.

Barry nudged Tom and pointed toward the mine entrance. Crouching, they slipped to the other side of the road and made their way toward it.

The shadows were much deeper inside the sheltered cavelike shack but there was no mistaking the huge yellow forklift standing to one side of the elevator shaft. The forklift convinced Barry that the canisters of gas, or at least one of them, was below in the mine. The hydraulic lift would have been used to transfer the cylinder from the truck to the elevator.

Raindrops plopped steadily into the gathering puddles near the entrance. Tom Radley took Barry's elbow. Turning, Barry looked in the direction Tom pointed. A man had come along the dark, shadowed structure that housed the mine elevator. A flashlight winked out as he looked. The man clicked a lighter under a cigarette.

Barry motioned and they drew back away from the entrance. "There's no way of telling if they've rigged up a telephone to the gallery, and they may have signals. The worst part is we won't know until we try to go down in the elevator."

"If the gas is down there, we wouldn't have a chance," Lobo said.

Tom said, "If we can take the guards, we may be able to figure a way to bring the others to the surface. There's no way they could move the canister on short notice."

"Is there another way out?" Lobo asked.

Barry shook his head. "Not unless they bored a new shaft someplace, and that would be too risky. These old mines are pretty shaky and any drilling could just as easily bring the whole roof in. I think we can rule out the possibility; they're bottled up down there. Yashar was counting on no one ever locating this spot."

"Then let's take them," Lobo said.

Barry rubbed his jaw. "We've no weapons—"

Tom said, "I've got a pistol."

"—but then, we don't want to make any noise. How many guards in the shed?"

"Two, I'd guess," Tom said.

"And one at the mine entrance. Can we neutralize all of them?"

Lobo grinned. "We can try."

Barry said, "I'll take the one at the entrance. You two take the others. Surprise 'em if you can. Tie them up."

"Right," Lobo nodded. "Let's go."

Barry walked into the mine entry confidently, making no effort to move soundlessly. He saw the dark shadow detach itself from the wall at his right. A voice said, "Is that you, Bert?"

Barry grunted, turning toward the man. He saw the glint of light on a rifle barrel. In another second he was close enough to see the other's eyes and the pale blur of a face. Barry struck out at the rifle, using the flat of his hand, hoping to knock it free with the first blow.

The man yelped in surprise but recovered quickly. The rifle barrel whipped around and Barry felt it slam against his side. He thrust out, connecting with the other's face, grabbing the barrel at the same time. The man grunted and fell backward against the wall. Barry expected the rifle to fire but it did not.

He got both hands on the weapon, twisting it violently. He felt the barrel strike bone with a harsh, grating sound. The man moaned and dropped heavily. Barry was left standing over the man with the rifle in his hands.

It was a Winchester, lever action. Barry found the flashlight the man had used and put it between his knees, switching it on. He cracked the breach; there was no shell in the chamber of the rifle. No wonder the man had not fired it. Levering it, he let the hammer down and stood the rifle against the wall.

He clicked the flash off and went to the entrance. He could see the light flickering in the shed. In a moment, a dark form came across the empty shale toward him. It was Lobo.

"Piece of cake, Barry. They're both tied and gagged."

"Let's get this one tied."

Lobo pulled a length of cord from his pocket and bent over the fallen man while Barry held the light.

Tom Radley came behind him. "There's a car coming."

Chapter Seventeen

They picked up the groaning man and carried him quickly outside and around the side of the building. Barry darted back to the entry and grabbed the rifle.

The car came up the grade slowly and pulled into the clearing near the parked truck and blue Thunderbird. The headlights glowed, went off for a second, then on and off again rapidly. The car engine was switched off and someone called out as the car door opened.

The three stepped back into the shadows. Lobo said in a low voice, "They won't find the two we trussed up . . ."

Barry could hear small sounds over the patter of the rain. The occupants of the car were heading for the mine entrance. Thunder rumbled in the skies above, echoing among the hills menacingly.

Three figures came out of the gloom. One of them had a flashlight; the beam jerked this way and that, the cold light showing misty drops and dark puddles. As the three entered the doorway, Barry saw Freda Polk's face clearly. He felt Lobo stiffen beside him. "What the hell—!"

At Tom's questioning look, Barry said, "Freda Polk, the agitator."

Barry moved toward the entrance cautiously. The woman and two men inside were talking but he could not distinguish words. Probably they were discussing the lack of guards. He heard the whirr of machinery and the clanging of steel as the cage stopped. A further sound as the metal gate slid back.

What the hell was Freda doing here? Barry's men had not been able to find any connection between her and the militant Yashar group. Barry knew Freda was sympathetic to the National Liberation Army but he had not expected a direct alliance. Maybe he was wrong.

The door slid into place with a clang and the metallic whirr started. The cage was moving down into the mine.

Barry moved around the corner into the entrance. He heard Tom Radley's warning, "Wait—" He saw the shadows move and realized suddenly that all three of the newcomers had not gone down into the mine. His instincts warned him at the last instant. Barry whirled as something came seeking his skull. He ducked, moving into his attacker with an arm up to ward off a second blow. He could hear the creak and hum of the mine elevator and the muted throbs of a generator. He heard Lobo's voice swearing.

A flashlight clicked on. Barry saw the man with whom he was grappling, a medium-tall, husky youngster with long hair. He sidestepped a vicious kick and drove a right hand into the other's face. As the man fell, Barry hit him twice more.

In the next instant he was clubbed from behind.

Barry fought the rising blackness. He felt the harsh scrape of the gritty soil on his cheek and tried to open his eyes. He could hear Lobo's continuing grumble. Someone else was talking. A brilliant light swept his face and Barry grimaced at the pain that seared his eyeballs. The light moved from its direct path on him and he opened his eyes. His head was clearing rapidly though the pain remained throbbing behind his ear.

Lobo was on the ground next to him, half sitting up and rubbing a spot on his temple where blood seeped from a livid bruise. Barry squinted, shielding his eyes from the light.

Freda Polk's voice said to him, "You never know when to quit, do you?" She sounded cold and hard.

Barry tried to sit up. The man he had felled was still crumpled on the floor of the entrance, with another man leaning over him. There was no sign of Tom Radley.

"Stay where you are," Freda said. When she moved he saw the revolver pointed at him. "What the hell are you doing here?" There was still a measure of surprise in her voice.

"I could ask you the same question." Barry glanced at the entrance, dripping with rain. Was Tom out there, watching the action?

"You know damned well what I'm doing here." Freda waved the flash around, taking them all in.

"You're part of Yashar's group?" He wondered how she and her two companions had seen them—or had they merely taken routine precautions when they found the guards missing?

"I'm working for peace," Freda said, "nothing's changed. You're the one who doesn't belong. I don't know how you found this place but it's too late to worry about that. Ali Yashar will decide what to do with you."

Barry grunted, touching his head. It had been a glancing blow and he had never lost consciousness for more than a few seconds, yet it hurt like hell. Freda had obviously sent the empty elevator down as a warning. Would Yashar himself come roaring up with reinforcements?

He caught Lobo's eye and understood immediately that Lobo was better off than he pretended. The two men who had arrived with Freda were still to one side, one of them administering to the other. Barry moved as if to rise.

"Don't try anything," Freda said, a note of hysteria

creeping into her voice. "I know how to use this gun." She stepped back.

"I came to talk to Yashar again," Barry said—which was close to the truth. "We had a meeting—"

"*You* had a meeting with Yashar?!" She didn't believe him. "You expect me to believe that? You're exactly what Yashar and the rest of us are fighting against. You're part of the other side—you don't give a damn about anything but your own precious world."

"Why don't you ask Yashar?"

She wasn't listening. "You want to control the world even more than you do now. Well, it's coming to an end, rich boy. The final reckoning is on the way. The Establishment is all washed up, only it doesn't know it. The people are taking over. You've pushed us around long enough. We're through fighting your lousy commercial wars for you, and dying for you, and lining *your* pockets."

Barry laughed. "You're fighting for peace? With a madman ready to release deadly nerve gas into helpless cities if his demands aren't met?"

"That isn't true!" she yelled.

"It's what Yashar himself says. Think, Freda. Can't you see you're only a pawn? He'll use anyone who will help him get what he wants."

"All he wants is for your Establishment to release a few prisoners."

"And one of those prisoners is an expert in the use of nerve gas. Did you know that, Freda?"

She blinked at him. "You're just talking—you'd say anything, Barry, to get your way. That's your specialty, isn't it—sweet talk. If you can't steal it or buy it, then you can always talk your way—"

"Freda, for God's sake, make sense! What has Yashar promised you?"

She glared at him, then relaxed and brushed the

stringy blonde hair back from her cheek. In the harsh light of the torch Barry saw the excitement on her face. "He understands," she said fiercely. "He really understands what we're doing. He knows we can bring peace to the world and he's going to help . . . not just sit around and rap or make empty promises, but really help!"

"How is he going to help?" Barry wanted to keep her talking. Lobo was ready now, like a coiled spring. Had he spotted Tom Radley? There was still no sound from the elevator.

"He's going to set up a world peace organization. We will stop aggression wherever it erupts. Limit arms and outlaw bombs—"

"With blackmail? By threatening to use the nerve gas if nations don't comply? Freda, there are many peace organizations now. Millions of people want peace as much as you do."

She snorted. "But none of them are willing to do anything to stop Big Brother. They won't give up their investment in war. You and your kind have had your chance, Barry. Now it's ours."

Barry spoke slowly. "Yashar has already caused the deaths of dozens of people—and hundreds of injured are in hospitals. Does that sound to you as if he's trying to end death and destruction?"

Freda's eyes glittered. "He didn't order those deaths! Accidents, mistakes by stupid people in a hurry. If the government had released the prisoners in the first place none of it would have happened. If Jos—" She broke off and turned away.

"If Josef Draggett had been freed it would have been different?" Barry saw her quick look. She knew the name of the chemical warfare specialist. "Freda, we're both working for the same thing—can't you see that Yashar isn't on either side? None of his demands have mentioned peace."

170

"What did you say in this so-called meeting you had with him?"

"He asked me to act as intermediary, to contact the White House and convince the President Yashar was serious. That was just before the nerve gas was released off the Virginia coast. I met Yashar in a farmhouse in Pennsylvania. Shall I describe it for you?"

Her eyes were wary.

Barry sketched the place quickly, dredging his memory for details, describing Yashar, his mannerisms and his voice. He could see she was impressed. He said, "Yashar wants power. He's been repulsed in Kushka. His only chance is to blackmail this country. Can't you see he's willing to promise anything in order to gain what he wants? And that thing is power for himself. What good is his word? He set a deadline but he released gas and killed many people long before the time was up. He made no arrangements for his demand to be met. What good are his promises?"

"It was an accident," she said hotly. "He told me so himself."

From the corner of his eye Barry saw Lobo shift position. He kept Freda's attention riveted on himself. "Then what about your father?" he asked. "Yashar used him . . ."

She came close to him suddenly, eyes boring in. "What about my father? What do you know about that?" Hysteria had crept back into her tone. She was within arm's reach.

Barry saw the man behind Freda glance at them with interest. The supine man was conscious, struggling to sit up. Both of them looked like Freda's cohorts in the Peace Movement. Had they been sucked into Yashar's plans by Freda's enthusiasm?

"Your father was killed by Yashar—or one of his men—because Jeremiah Polk was hard to control. Yashar used your father to stir up a panic. Then, when his usefulness was over he was silenced so he couldn't reveal who had put him up to it."

She came at him in a rush. "You bastard! Your rotten Establishment killed him. He never had a chance!" She dived at Barry, striking out with the flashlight, forgetting the pistol for a moment.

Barry knocked the flash from her hands. It rolled along the ground. In an instant he had the pistol, wrenching it from her grasp, rolling her to the dirt, avoiding her hands. He heard Lobo rush the others as he fought off Freda. She swore at him in a steady chatter, kicking and clawing. It would have been easy to punch her unconscious but he resisted. It took him a minute to fend off her desperate lunges, then get her turned and helpless in an armlock.

When he was able to look around, Tom Radley was there. He and Lobo had the two men on the ground. Lobo was tying their hands.

Tom said, "What'll we do with the wildcat?"

Barry pocketed the pistol. He pulled Freda to her feet, motioning Lobo to tie her hands.

The elevator motor hummed back to life.

"Someone's on the way up," Tom said. "Now what?"

"Douse the light," Barry hissed. "Let's get out of the entrance." He motioned Lobo to take Freda to one side out of possible danger. Tom Radley got the two men on their feet; he had disarmed them and given one of their pistols to Lobo.

"Move out to the road," Barry told them, "and keep going."

The long-haired man supported his friend. They did not argue. With a glance at Freda, they did as they were told.

There was a light in the elevator as it rose to the surface. Barry chewed his lip. It was likely that Yashar and his men would be on the lift, probably armed and ready for trouble. He had no desire to shoot down any of

172

them. How could they avoid it?

Barry could see into the mine entrance past the yellow fork lift. The whirr of machinery stopped, the mesh gate clanged open and four men stepped out. The leader was the huge figure of Ali Yashar. There was a light on in the open framework of the elevator, and one of Yashar's companions carried a large torch which he flashed around the entrance.

Yashar himself carried a submachine gun.

As the four stepped off the elevator, Barry called out, "Yashar—it's Hewes-Bradford. I want to talk."

Yashar halted instantly; his face showed surprise. Then the burp gun came up menacingly. Yashar frowned toward the spot he thought the sound had come from. "Show yourself, my friend."

Two of Yashar's companions said something in low tones and Yashar replied in his own tongue. Instantly the others spread out, pistols held ready.

Freda screamed out then, "Yashar—there're only three of them!"

Lobo quickly stifled her, swearing under his breath.

Yashar chuckled. "So, Mr. Hewes-Bradford, we're surrounded, is that it—by three men?" He moved his head and the men with him advanced slowly. The man with the torch put it on the ground, the beam shining toward the entrance. "Step out, my friend. Let me see you, then we'll talk."

Barry said nothing. His hunch told him that if he stepped out, Yashar would pull the trigger.

He gritted his teeth. In another half dozen steps Yashar would be at the entrance and, despite the night and the rain, would be able to spot them. And Yashar had the chopper. The odds were in his favor. The only hope was to keep him and his men bottled inside the entry.

Barry aimed the pistol through a crack in the wooden sidewall and squeezed the trigger. The torch exploded.

All four men jumped and one of them loosed off a round that went whining into the night. Barry's second shot clanged off a steel upright in the elevator shaft, missing the naked bulb there by an inch.

Ali Yashar's submachine gun chattered. The muzzle blast flared and heavy caliber bullets shredded the edge of the doorway as Barry jumped back.

The three others fired as well, aiming blindly. A fusillade of bullets tore the night open, thudding into the opposite hillside.

Barry fired three times more, over the heads of the men inside the entrance. The lead shrieked, rapped into rotting timbers, and ricocheted off steel supports. Yashar's chopper stuttered, seeking him out. Splinters flew and wood was chewed to bits. Then everyone was firing at once. Barry got down on one knee, reloading the pistol. It sounded for a few seconds like a full scale battle.

Suddenly it stopped.

In that moment of silence, Freda screamed again, elbowed herself free of Lobo, and ran to the mine entrance. But the men inside were jumpy and the guns swung toward her.

"Don't! Don't shoot!" Freda waved her arms and began to walk toward the elevator shaft and the light. "Let me help—I'm—we're on the same side—"

Yashar's voice was an ugly sound. "You brought them here! You are a traitor!"

"No—!!"

Yashar's chopper stuttered and Freda collapsed, shot to bits. Red blood pooled, a darker stain on the dark earth.

Silence fell again, as Barry stared horrified. He heard the four of them talking, muttering angrily—then the steel gate clanged.

Yashar roared, "Hewes-Bradford—do you hear me?"

"I hear you, Yashar."

"The deadline has expired. My demands have not been met."

"Give yourself up, Yashar. You're finished."

Yashar's voice became angry, "Yashar is never—"

"Now you're killing your friends, Yashar. That girl came here to help you."

"She was a traitor!"

"You can't get out of there alive. You're finished."

Yashar's voice became almost hysterical. "The nerve gas will be released as I told you! It is in place now, this very instant. At my command it will be released in the center of Washington! Everyone will die!"

Barry heard the whirr of the elevator machinery.

Tom said, "He's going down into the mine again."

Chapter Eighteen

Barry whirled, yelling at Tom, "Get that lantern from the shed!"

Tom waved, sprinting off, feet slapping through puddles of inky black water. Barry hurried toward the dark shaft where the elevator had vanished below the surface. The cables creaked, wheels shrilling because of lack of grease, and the motor noise echoed in the headframe.

Lobo shouted, "Hurry up with the light—"

"Let's find a way to cut off the power," Barry said, glancing round the shaft and probing with the flashlight beam. They could easily destroy the lines but they might have need of the elevator later.

Tom returned with two lanterns, handing one to Barry who lifted it high. A thick cable led from the main shaft and disappeared into darkness.

Barry indicated the cable, glancing at Tom. "Follow it and see if you can turn off the generator."

"Right," Tom said. He worked his way around the shaft opening and began tracing the cable. Lobo took the lantern from Barry and went out to the entrance where Freda's body still lay in the misty rain. Barry followed, frowning down at the murdered girl. The body had sustained such a blast from the submachine gun that he feared to move it . . . lest they discover it was cut in half. Shaking his head, Barry mopped the rain from his face.

"I'll find a tarp, if there's one around," Lobo said.

They returned to the shaft entrance. Lobo took a flashlight and prowled in a shed while Barry studied the headframe and the moving cable. Far below, the elevator came to a halt. The generator cut out and it was still. Only the monotonous plop of rain into puddles broke the silence. Yashar and his men had reached the main gallery.

The light bobbed as Tom retraced his steps. "There's a main switch," he said, grinning. "At least we know Yashar can't surprise us. Unless he climbs the ladder he's going to stay down there till we let him up."

Barry nodded. It was a hell of a long haul to the surface climbing the vertical ladder.

Lobo came out of the shed with a tarpaulin that was thickly folded and obviously years old. He shook it out, finding it ragged and worn through in long strips. But it was the best they had. He put it over the body. It made a pitiful lump on the soggy earth.

Tom held the lantern over the elevator shaft. Barry frowned thoughtfully into the black maw. "I think it's time we got back into contact with the world. Tom, why don't you get down to one of the cars and drive out to a phone. Call Frank Trask and ask him to get an Army Chem Warfare expert out here. Tell him the situation—anything he wants to know. Right?"

Tom nodded. "Frank'll have the Army and the Marines as well as the cops crowding around." He handed the lantern over.

"I won't mind that," Barry said. "We need all the help we can get."

"I'll take the kid's T-bird," Tom said. "It'll save a minute." He ran through the rain toward the blue car.

Barry hung the lantern on a wire and steadied it from swinging. Wild shadows were racing around the mine entrance. As he watched Tom get into the car, lights blazed suddenly as another car crested the hill.

177

"Who's that?" Lobo said, staring at the distant headlights. "More of the gang?"

Barry drew back, motioning Lobo to get behind cover. The approaching car splashed along the narrow track, passing the T-bird and the truck without slowing. Someone was in a hurry. The newcomer bounced over the rutted ground, skidding in the mud, back wheels spinning as the engine roared. The driver was unused to the muddy dirt roads, Barry thought, watching the car pull up the steep grade of the final approach. The car ground to a halt, the engine was switched off, and the driver emerged.

Lobo said, "Only one . . ." He drew back the hammer of his pistol.

"Let's take him alive," Barry said. He raised the flashlight as the figure nearly fell over Freda Polk's body and came on to the mine entrance. As Barry switched on the light, Lobo exclaimed in astonishment. It was Elorith Modan.

Elorith stopped short, staring at the sudden light. Barry went forward, took her arm, and led her inside out of the rain. She looked very frightened. Her face glistened with rain and her lips trembled. For a moment she seemed confused, then alarmed at seeing Barry and Lobo.

"Ohhh—I didn't—"

Barry said, "We weren't exactly expecting you!"

"I—I—" She stared at him. "How did you find this place?" Without waiting for an answer, she turned, staring at the body under the sodden tarp. "Who—who is that?" She pressed a hand to her throat.

"Freda Polk." Barry watched the woman closely. If Elorith was on Yashar's side he wanted to know it. He said, "Yashar killed her with a burp gun." It might shake Elorith up to discover how ruthless Yashar was.

She turned her face away, lips tightly compressed.

She was shuddering. Barry drew her farther inside the entrance, out of the cold breeze that blew fitfully, flinging raindrops into their faces.

"Why are you here, Elorith?"

"I—I learned that Yashar is here."

"How did you know?"

"A man—Ceri. He was one of Yashar's first converts. He came to me when he discovered how unstable Ali had become." She looked at him. "He *is* here, isn't he?"

Barry nodded, indicating the shaft. "He's down below in the mine."

"I came to t-talk to him."

He was surprised. "Talk? What can you talk about?"

"Barry, he's insane—he will not keep the promises he makes!"

"Then what good is your talking to him?" Was Elorith telling the truth? She had known about the mine yet she had said nothing to the authorities. Could he trust her? He watched her walk away and come back, obviously agitated.

She said, "One of Yashar's men, one who helped put the poison gas in the boat off Virginia, came to me for help. He could not take part in Yashar's plans any longer."

"What kind of help?"

Elorith sighed. "He wanted money so he can go away where Yashar can't reach him." She took Barry's hand. "I swear to you I knew nothing of this place until Ceri told me. I rushed here hoping to—" She stopped. "I don't know what I hoped. I only know Yashar must be prevented from doing any more harm." She started toward the dark shaft.

Barry said, "Elorith!"

She turned. "How does one get down there, by an elevator?"

"Yes. But it's at the bottom of the shaft now. You can't go down there, Elorith. Nothing you say is going to mean anything to him."

She sighed again and looked at him strangely. "Yes, you are right." She let her breath out and seemed to slump. Avoiding Barry's gaze, she stared at the murky cavity of the main shaft. "He has a canister of nerve gas down there." Her tone was flat and lifeless.

"You're sure?"

"Yes. Ceri told me. He has seen it."

"One cylinder only?" Barry knew he had been hoping this was the end of the trail, that all four gas cylinders were here. It was a vain hope.

"Yes." Elorith opened her large shoulder purse and dug in it to bring out a handkerchief. Turning away, she dabbed at her eyes. Barry glanced at Lobo and shrugged slightly. There was little they could do now but get Elorith to return to her hotel. He glanced out toward the hills, seeing the glow of the T-bird's headlights as Tom Radley drove from the area.

Elorith walked slowly toward the shaft—then she moved swiftly, stepping forward and taking something from the bag. Before either Barry or Lobo could react, she tossed it into the shaft. Barry darted to her but she had a second grenade out, pulled the pin and flung it into the dark pit.

Yelling, Barry whirled her away and into Lobo's arms. "She's got grenades!"

Lobo half carried her out of the entry, with Barry on their heels. Lobo tossed the purse to Barry; he went through it quickly but there were no other grenades in it.

The two explosions came within seconds of each other. Two dull booms, deep in the mineshaft, vibrated the headframe. Nothing else happened for a half moment, then the shock wave came up, jiggling the lantern

180

on the forklift and bringing dust and the smell of cordite with it.

Barry swore. There wasn't a hell of a lot of explosive power in a couple of grenades but the shock waves they would set up below, in weakened structures and confined areas, might do enormous damage. He already could hear a distant rumbling following the blasts. Smoke and dust continued to boil out of the shaft.

"Jesus! The canister!" Lobo said, staring at Barry.

"Let's hope it was far enough back from the shaft." Barry was surprised at the calmness Elorith displayed. "That was a foolish thing to do. The whole damn mine is falling in down below."

The rumbling grew louder and dust, smelling of damp and of coal, belched up. Barry said, "Let's move out of here." He grabbed the lantern and Lobo hurried Elorith toward the parked car.

"Wait a sec," Barry said. "What was that?"

"That damned gas is odorless and colorless," Lobo shouted. "We'd better make tracks!" He opened the door of Elorith's car and shoved her into it.

Barry turned back, holding the lantern high. It sounded like a voice. Was someone still alive in the mine? He ran back toward the elevator shaft and the voice came again, a loud cry, a call of pure desperation.

Lobo yelled at him, "Barry!"

Barry said, "Someone's alive down there." He hung the lantern by the shaft.

"Barry—for Godsakes!"

"If the guy can yell there can't be any gas escaping." Barry leaned over the steel railing, peering down. The dust was definitely thinning. The sounds of collapsing tunnels had ceased for the moment. He heard the groans again.

Lobo ran to him. "This entire thing can cave in any minute, Barry!"

Barry doffed his coat. "Someone's trying to climb out. Maybe he's hurt—"

"You can't go down there!" Lobo sounded horrified.

"The hell I can't." He swung a leg over the railing and stopped. Elorith ran into the entrance—but she had nothing in her hands.

"What is it?"

Lobo growled, "There's someone down there. We can't make out what he's saying."

She leaned over the shaft, head cocked. Then she straightened. "I think it's Ali. He's muttering in Arabic . . . something about his arm." She pulled at Barry. "Leave him there—I am only sorry I didn't kill him. He doesn't deserve to live!"

Barry watched her eyes. "You mean you came here to kill him?"

"Someone who can get close to him must do it! He is a madman. Even his own people are leaving him as they realize what he is doing. He cares nothing for the lives of others! Anyone who gets in his way will be shot or worse." She glanced into the shaft. "Let him die!"

Barry said, "I can't. He's the only one who knows where the other canisters are."

"That's not true." She shook her dark head. "I know also . . . Ceri has told me."

Barry's look said he doubted it and Elorith's oval face took on a kind of fierceness. "Ceri was one of the close few. He knew the location of each canister and the plan. His information was my price for helping him!"

Barry felt a brief moment of relief. She was telling the truth—he was sure of it. The crisis was over. They had only to notify the authorities and the canisters would be recovered. It was over—except for the man in the shaft below them.

He turned to Lobo. "I'm going down to bring Yashar up."

"Barry! Let me do it!" Lobo tried to stop him.

"No—" Barry swung over the railing and jumped at the ladder nailed to the wall. He went down it with an agility he did not feel. He wished to hell he had a rope tied about his waist.

The dust choked him; it was settling but still thick. It gritted between his teeth and he had to squint to see the black wall in front of him. Below, Yashar still groaned, muttering to himself. Barry climbed down steadily; the ladder was in good repair, very solid. Some of the rungs had sharp edges as if they had been replaced not long past. The feeble lantern light did not reach here at all. He could see it glowing far above but he had to feel in the void for each step.

Barry had to stop now and then, press his face to his shirt to breathe, then go on. The smell from the mine was very strong. How far down was Yashar?

When his foot struck something finally and a sharp cry came from close by, he knew he had found Yashar. He said quickly, "I've come to help you." The man might be partly out of his head, reach for a weapon—

"Arm, arm—caught in the ladder. I think it is broken—"

Barry slid sideways, pushing past the other, feeling in the inky darkness for the arm. There was really not room for both of them on the ladder; a flashlight would have simplified matters but he couldn't help that now. The side of the shaft had broken away and the ladder had been partially splintered by a weakening of the heavy timbers that had fallen.

Yashar groaned loudly as Barry probed cautiously. The arm seemed bent at an unnatural angle. It was held between the back of the ladder and a thick timber. Yashar cried out in agony as he felt Barry's fingers exploring.

A sudden crackling sound sliced through the darkness and was followed by a distant roar. Vibrations shook the shaft. Rotting wood shoring was giving way in forgotten tunnels.

"Hang on," Barry gritted. "The arm will come out but it'll hurt."

"Hurry—" Yashar groaned.

Barry levered the timber away. It fell, clattering against the sides of the shaft, then silence till it slammed into debris far below. The elevator must be covered with tons of dirt and rock, Barry realized.

He freed the arm, biting his lip as he felt naked bone. Yashar groaned again, jerking convulsively as the waves of pain hit him. Barry was afraid the man would black out and drop away. But he did not.

Barry put the arm down at Yashar's side; he had no way to tie it and he found himself clenching his jaws, knowing the intense pain the other must be suffering. Yashar was breathing hard and sweating, holding onto the ladder with superhuman effort.

Barry waited a moment, "Can you move now?"

"I—I think so—" If he knew who was helping him he gave no sign.

"I'll be right behind you," Barry said. "Just slide up holding on to the upright—take it slow and easy."

Yashar grunted, moving, resting, and moving again. It was agonizingly slow work, climbing out that way. Barry gave the man what support he could, wishing a thousand times more for a rope. It was stifling in the shaft and there were times in the long haul that he felt like a man in a dream, climbing in blackness toward nothing, coming from nothing. And he knew that Yashar must feel worse.

After what seemed an eternity he heard Lobo's voice from above. "Are you all right, Barry?"

"Yes—" The single word brought on a spasm of coughing.

Then somehow Lobo was hauling Yashar out and Barry opened his eyes to see the lantern light close by. He clambered up the last rungs of the ladder into wel-

184

come air; his hands were torn and lacerated by the rough wood. Yashar was huddled against the wall of the entrance, holding the shattered arm.

"God, Barry—I thought you'd had it!" Lobo sounded as if he'd held his breath the whole time.

Yashar's face and clothes were streaked with coal dust and grime; his eyes were wild with pain. He stared at Barry without speaking.

Barry said, "There's no one else alive down there?"

Yashar shook his head. He was still breathing hard. "I was climbing the ladder when the explosions came. The others were caught at the bottom." He looked from one to the other of them. "Why did you throw the explosives?"

"We didn't," Lobo said. "What about the canister?"

Yashar stared at him a long moment. "Buried in the rubble." The dark eyes glinted and he looked away. He peered at the car parked outside. Elorith was inside, staring at him. Yashar grunted; if he saw her he made no other sign.

"Let's get to a doctor," Barry said. He straightened Yashar. "We can make a sling for the arm."

Chapter Nineteen

Elorith pushed into the corner of the front seat as Lobo entered the back of the car, following Yashar. Barry slid behind the wheel. No one spoke. Elorith gave the injured man one swift look and sat very still, head down.

Yashar, jaws working, still dripping sweat despite the chill, sat holding the arm, his eyes closed. He braced himself with both feet against the roll of the car as Barry backed it and drove slowly over the uneven ground to the road. The rain poured down, pattering on the roof of the car. The windshield wipers clacked monotonously.

It was over. Barry glanced at the man in the back; there were so many questions he wanted to ask Yashar. They would have to wait. They would be much too late to intercept the message Tom Radley had by this time phoned to Frank Trask to be relayed to the authorities. Troops, FBI, and police were probably screaming over the roads on their way to the mine. They would be able to get the locations of the remaining gas canisters from Elorith. So much had happened in a few days.

Barry was concentrating on the immediate future when Yashar spoke. His voice was thick and heavy. "You are a fool, Hewes-Bradford."

Barry glanced in the rear view mirror but Yashar's face was only a pale blur. The man's voice was cold and detached when he spoke again, "Yes, you are a fool—"

"Why do you think so?" Apparently Yashar had overcome his panic and was suppressing the pain. Was

186

he running yet another bluff? Barry glanced at Elorith. She was staring out the window at the rain.

Yashar said, "I still have three canisters of gas."

For a moment no one spoke. Then Barry smiled at the blur of face. "We know where the others are, Yashar. You are finished, as I told you before. The military will have them all by this time tomorrow."

Yashar pushed forward slightly, wincing as the movement obviously brought him pain. "How could you know? You are lying. The canisters are in safe places—you will never find them. This instant my men are waiting for my call. If they do not hear from me quickly the gas will be released in Washington, D.C.!"

Lobo pushed the excited man back into the seat. "All right, cool it, Yashar."

Barry stared at the road, twin puddles of brown water in the headlights. Yashar was bluffing again. The prisoners were in Washington—the men he had tried so desperately to free.

Elorith said softly, "It is not true. Ali was counting on Josef Draggett to take charge of the gas. His men are frightened since the accident on the boat. None of them will touch the canisters."

Yashar lunged suddenly, striking out with his big fist at the back of Elorith's head. She made a small sound and slumped forward as the blow struck. Lobo grabbed Yashar and slammed him back against the seat as Barry applied the brakes, skidding the car. But Elorith was not hurt. She sat up, face pale and angry in the dim light of the car; her black eyes sparking.

Barry asked, "Are you all right?"

Nodding, she opened her purse and found a handkerchief. Barry put the car in gear again and turned his attention back to the winding road. They passed the spot where they'd left the rented Plymouth. Someone could return for it later.

Then, from a corner of his eyes he saw Elorith reach

into the glove compartment and he caught the flicker of metal. He slammed on the brakes again but the sound of the shot exploded inside the car. Elorith was half across the seat, a small revolver in her hand, thumbing the hammer to get a second shot at the man in the corner.

Lobo jumped with the quickness of a striking rattler, grabbing the muzzle of the gun, twisting it to get it away from her. Elorith struggled, her body taut and hard, feet kicking. Barry had to fight the wheel as the car slewed sideways in the mud.

Elorith was screaming, "He does not deserve to live! He is an enemy to your country and mine!"

But Lobo got the gun away from her and it thudded on the floor.

Then the door opened and a cold blast of rain and wind came into the car. As Barry brought the car to a halt he saw Yashar tumbling from the seat, diving into the darkness.

Lobo was swearing. "Barry—he got the pistol!"

Barry yanked the brake and slid out of the driver's seat in one motion. He slammed the door; Yashar was a moving blur in the woods ahead of him.

"He's got the gun!" Lobo yelled again.

"Stay with her," Barry said and began to run. The cold rain soaked him before he had gone ten steps. He dug into the pocket of the jacket for the pistol he'd taken from Freda. He saw Yashar slow, then turn. A yellow-white blast appeared in the night and was whipped away as Barry heard the pistol shot. The bullet rapped into a tree nearby.

He swore under his breath. This was not what he wanted. He wanted to deliver a whole, live Yashar to the authorities. He couldn't risk losing him now. Barry ran at the man knowing that if Yashar put any distance between them it might be impossible to find him in the dark.

A second shot whined over his head and Barry ducked instinctively. Yashar was firing at sounds; it was too dark to aim properly. Barry paused, hearing nothing but the slap of the rain. Yashar had halted and was waiting for him, pistol cocked. He could hear the sound of the car behind on the road; the engine was ticking over, wipers clacking. He slid behind a thick boled tree.

Then Lobo gunned the car and backed it, sending the twin headlight beams into the trees. It was a move born of desperation and might have done Barry more harm than good. But Barry froze.

Yashar was caught in the beams, the revolver thrust out. He fired a quick shot at the headlights.

Barry shouted, "Drop the gun, Yashar!"

Yashar answered with a roar. He charged in the direction of Barry's voice. A shot splintered a branch only inches above Barry's head.

Barry fired. Yashar's hand went up and the big man halted, skidding, sliding; the pistol dropped and Yashar turned as if in slow motion. Then he collapsed in the weeds, face upward, glistening with rain.

Counting off a dozen seconds before moving, Barry slid between the trees. He heard Lobo's voice calling, the sound of rapid footsteps. But Yashar was finished. Barry knelt and felt the man's neck for a pulse. There was none.

Lobo, breathing hard, halted beside him. "Are you all right?"

"Not hurt," Barry said, straightening. Yashar's eyes were open, staring at nothing. The rain spattered the dark irises.

Epilogue

Barry strode across the wide flagstone terrace, hands deep in pockets as he gazed over the blue Pennsylvania hills that fell away into the distances below Hewesridge. The air was warmer this morning and smelled fresh and sweet with a spring that had finally emerged.

Yashar was dead; the canisters of deadly nerve gas had all been recovered intact. What was left of his gang was in jail.

Elorith had been right about Yashar's bluff—there had been no preparations to release the gas in Washington. Barry had been on the phone only an hour ago, talking to General Harry Fontaine. The General informed him that Chemical Warfare was in the process of neutralizing the collapsed mine shaft with strong caustics. They would then complete the cave-in and bury the canister forever.

He turned as Elorith opened the French doors that led to the dining room. She smiled and breathed deeply. "You must think me lazy, getting up at this hour. I am normally an early riser."

"You've had an exhausting time these last few days." Barry took her arm and led her to the balustrade. Holden came from the dining room with a tray which he set on a wrought iron table. He arranged cups and a silver coffee pot and departed.

Elorith's face clouded. "I'm glad it's over. To think I once believed I loved Ali . . ." She shook her head. "Was I so wrong or did Ali change that much?"

"There's no way of knowing. Maybe a little of each. He saw a way to grab great power—and you know what that's done to better men."

"He was so sure, so dedicated. I believed—we all believed—he was working for the good of our people." She looked away, staring at the horizon.

Barry glanced around. "Let's have some coffee, shall we?" He went to the table. "As soon as an individual gets the idea he can control an entire nation and bend it to his will, there's trouble. The taste of power those canisters gave Yashar was his undoing. He forgot the cause that had initiated the whole plan and went overboard in his own interests. He didn't care who was killed in his rush for power. He used Freda Polk and her father and when they were no longer useful he disposed of them. He would have done the same to you—" He stopped, alarmed by the stricken expression on her face.

"But—but he must have known his bid for power in Kushka had failed! His people, the Liberation Army, scattered like frightened chickens when the Shah opposed them."

Barry nodded. "Yes, but to back down in this country after he had made his threats would have been more defeat than he could bear. Probably he refused to believe the reports from Kushka . . . and he believed a triumph here would send him home a hero, give him another chance."

Elorith turned away, sighing deeply. "It was kind of you to bring me here. It's so peaceful."

"I thought we should know each other better." He poured the coffee and tasted it.

She smiled, seeming to put aside thoughts of the past days. "Will you come with me to Kushka? My uncle will be so pleased to see you again."

He handed her a cup. "It crossed my mind—a vacation will do us both good."

"A vacation?"

"Call it an extended journey, to cleanse our minds. We can make Kushka the first stop."

"The two of us?"

"Well, and Kel Grodin, the pilot. But he'll be no trouble. He's got a girl in every city. What do you say?"

She put down the coffee cup and moved closer. "I think it's a marvelous idea. When shall we go?"

"How about right after breakfast in the morning?"

6-74